Praise for Alexander McCall Smith and

My Italian Bulldozer

"This is McCall Smith's genius—he makes you love the people in his books. . . . That and he makes you laugh, and how many can claim that?" —*The New York Times*

"A delightful mixture of humor, humanity, and observation. Just as at home in Italy as he is in Botswana, McCall Smith depicts the people of Tuscany with verve." —*Country Life*

"[McCall Smith's] accomplished novels . . . [are] dependent on small gestures redolent with meaning and main characters blessed with pleasing personalities. . . . These novels are gentle probes into the mysteries of human nature." —*Newsday*

"Filled with delightfully farcical situations and intelligent and appealing, good-natured characters, *My Italian Bulldozer* is as memorable and pleasing as its beautiful Tuscan backdrop. Another praiseworthy concoction from the always dependable Alexander McCall Smith." —*Lancashire Evening Post*

"[McCall Smith] presents us with gentle stories that ask profound questions and leave us not with all the answers, but with a smile on our face and a lot more to think about than when we began."

—*New York Journal of Books*

"There's not a more charming author on the face of the Earth."   —*The Seattle Times*

Alexander McCall Smith

My Italian Bulldozer

Alexander McCall Smith is the author of the No. 1
Ladies' Detective Agency novels and a number of other
series and standalone books. His works have been trans-
lated into more than forty languages and have been
bestsellers throughout the world. He lives in Scotland.

www.alexandermccallsmith.com

My Italian Bulldozer

Alexander McCall Smith

Anchor Books
A Division of Penguin Random House LLC
New York

THIS BOOK IS FOR

William Dalrymple, author and historian

FIRST ANCHOR BOOKS EDITION, APRIL 2018

The Library of Congress has cataloged the Pantheon edition as follows:
McCall Smith, Alexander, [date] author.
Title: My Italian Bulldozer / Alexander McCall Smith.
LCSH: Authors — Fiction. Bulldozers — Fiction. Italy — Fiction.
BISAC: FICTION / Humorous. | FICTION / Literary. |
GSAFD: Humorous fiction
LCC PR6063.C326 M9 2017
DDC 823/.914—dc23
LC record available at lccn.loc.gov/2016037816

Anchor Books Trade Paperback ISBN: 978-1-101-97283-0
eBook ISBN: 978-1-101-87140-9

www.anchorbooks.com

Printed in the United States of America
10 9 8 7 6 5 4 3 2 1

My Italian Bulldozer

I

People Do Strange Things

It was the first time that Paul had made duck à l'orange for friends since Becky left him for her personal trainer. Her departure—after four years of living together—had been a surprise, but not as great a shock as the discovery of her new lover's identity. Looking back on it, Paul realised that all the signs had been there, and might so easily have been spotted. He felt a lingering, slightly reproachful regret: had he been less absorbed by his work, he might have noticed her indifference; had he given her more time, he might have been forewarned by her restlessness, by the occasional guilty, almost furtive look; but even had he picked this up, nothing could have prepared him for her choice of Tommy, the tattooed mesomorph with whom she suddenly went off to live.

"I didn't want this," he said to Gloria, his editor, trying as hard as he could to be stoical. "But it's happened. That's all there is to it, I suppose. People split up."

They were having coffee together in Gloria's kitchen when this conversation took place. Her office was in her flat, and Paul dropped in from time to time to see her, to collect proofs, to bounce ideas off her—or just to be listened to. She was good at that—she would make him a cup of the Assam tea he liked, sit on her sofa with her legs tucked under her, and let him talk. "No, go on," she would say if he asked her if he was wasting her time. "I like wasting time with you, Paul—you know that."

She was, he reflected, one of his closest friends, in a rather curious, slightly old-fashioned way. *Dependable Gloria,* he said to himself, *always there, always positive.* But in spite of their closeness, what did he know about her? That she was a freelance editor who lived in Edinburgh but who came from somewhere else originally—somewhere near Bristol, where she had gone to university. Her parents had both died when she was in her early twenties—she had told him about that—and she had no siblings. She was rather alone in the world, he imagined; there was an aunt she spoke about, and there were her friends in a hill-walking club. But apart from that did she have much of a social life? He had never really thought much about any of that. She was roughly his age—in her mid-thirties—and attractive in, well, a homely sort of way. She wore her hair short and she never used make-up. Yet she did not really need to, as her skin had that clear, almost translucent tone to it that one finds on the Celtic edges. Her mother, she had told him, was Irish, and that might explain the complexion. Rain-washed. Atlantic-blown. A friend of his had once described her as "worth a second look," but Paul, who had never seen her in that way, had simply nodded and said, "Yes, I suppose so."

But the most striking aspect of Gloria was her clothing. Paul had occasionally seen her dressed more formally—they sometimes attended book events together in London—but for the rest she seemed to be wedded to loose-fitting Indian print dresses, shifts that hung about her like light curtains. Somewhere behind the curtains was a figure, but he had never really seen it. There must be a mill somewhere in India, he thought, producing those designs almost exclusively for Gloria—she had

so many of them, in so many colours. He had once compli-
mented her on them, and she had beamed with pleasure, as if
he were the first man ever to say anything like that to her; perhaps he was, he thought.

And now that he needed somebody to talk to, of course
Gloria was there, and prepared to listen—as she always was.

She nodded sympathetically. "Yes, but the one left behind,
so to speak, always feels a bit raw? Who wouldn't?"

"Perhaps." He sought to reassure her, not wanting to be
thought self-pitying. "I'll get over it, of course."

"Good."

Gloria was about to say something else, but Paul continued, "Yet I can't help asking: Why *him*?"

Her eyes widened. She was pleased that Becky had left.
She was pleased because . . . She stopped herself. It was, she
feared, only too obvious. She was not in the least surprised
that Becky would go off with somebody . . . somebody less
intelligent than Paul. *The dark anarchic force of sex . . .* That
explained so much. "People do strange things. They fall for
the most unlikely people." She felt uncomfortable delving
any further, but she could understand why he wanted to
talk. "They just do. And listen, Paul; it's not your fault. Fault
doesn't come into it." She was not sure that this was quite
true; there were times when an inference of fault seemed
inescapable.

Paul sighed. "Have you actually seen them together?"

Gloria had. She had spotted the two of them entering a
supermarket hand in hand, and she could not help but notice
his pugilistic features—the broken nose, the vacuous expression, the rolling walk that only sailors and bodybuilders seem
to have. She had stared—discreetly, of course—but with a certain fascination.

"He's obviously very . . ." She searched for the word, and alighted upon *physical*. "Very *physical*." She uttered the word quietly, tentatively, as people do when they feel they might immediately have to retract what they have just said.

Paul nodded. "She met him in the gym," he said. "She started going there pretty regularly—sometimes twice a day. I should have realised that something was going on."

Gloria thought about this. It seemed to her that the gym was an odd place to conduct an affair. But perhaps not; perhaps there was something about the vaguely sweaty atmosphere of a gym that could set the heart racing. And people fell in love in all sorts of places; her friend Alice had fallen head over heels for a man she first met at the fish counter of her local supermarket. "I was examining a piece of halibut," she had said, "and I found myself looking at Tony, who was standing next to me. I just knew—right at that moment, I just knew."

"And all the time she was seeing him," continued Paul. "You would have thought there'd be a code of ethics forbidding personal trainers from having affairs with their clients. Psychotherapists have that sort of thing, don't they?"

Gloria nodded. "They do. They can't get involved with their clients, even if their clients fall in love with them— which I gather they often do. I gather they even expect it."

"Probably," said Paul, hesitantly. "But falling for one's therapist is surely entirely natural—of course we're going to fall in love with people who listen to us."

"Perhaps. So few do."

"Fall in love—or listen?"

She suspected that many people who appeared to be listening were in reality thinking about what they would say next. "Listen."

"And the relationship," Paul went on, "is not all that different—trainer and trainee, therapist and client. I could probably report him to his professional body, if I chose to."

For a moment she imagined a meeting of the personal trainers' professional body—a stern committee of the egregiously fit, all muscle, all glowing with health, conducting their business while running on the spot and lifting weights, the secretary taking the minutes while perched on an exercise bicycle.

Paul blushed. "No, I didn't mean to say that. I'm not feeling bitter." He hesitated. "She might come back, of course."

She looked grave. "Paul, once somebody runs away with somebody . . . somebody like that, she's unlikely to return." She thought of a friend, an art historian, who had fallen for a professional tennis player whose only topic of conversation was tennis. She had been blissfully happy, which was not the outcome that many had predicted—or wished for, for that matter: we do not want those of our friends who embark on adventures to get away with it. She remembered Vidal's famous comment—so waspish and at the same time so true—*every time one of my friends succeeds, I die a little.*

Paul was staring at the floor. *I don't need her,* he thought. *He's welcome to her. Tommy. Tommy and Becky. Oh, God . . .* He wanted to cry. He wanted to utter her name and sob.

The moment passed. "*La donna è mobile,*" he muttered. "Where does that come from again? You know . . . *La donna . . . something, something, something.*"

"Verdi," said Gloria. "*Rigoletto,* if I remember correctly. *La donna è mobile, qual piuma al vento, muta d'accento e di pensiero . . .* Of course, you speak Italian, don't you? Didn't you live there once?"

"For two years. In Florence. I was a student." He thought

back to that time—the period of greatest happiness in his life; to be twenty, in Florence, with no commitments and with a sense that life would always be like this, as golden, as full of possibilities.

"So no translation is necessary."

"Woman is fickle," he mused. "Like a feather in the wind, changes in voice and thought . . . So true."

Gloria disagreed—with Verdi and with Paul. "Not at all. More men leave women than the other way round. Everybody knows that."

"Are you sure? Or is that just what women want to believe?"

"No, it's absolutely true. There have been studies . . ." She waved a hand vaguely; she thought there probably had been, although chapter and verse were not always at hand when one needed them.

"*La donna è mobile* sounds nice," she continued, "but is utterly false, as so many operatic themes are."

Paul returned to the subject of the personal trainer. "I met him once or twice, you know. I went along to the gym with her and watched him taking her through her paces." He winced at the painful memory. "He stood very close to her, and every so often he would put a hand around her biceps and smile encouragingly."

"Oh dear."

Paul sighed. "What do they talk about, I wonder?"

Gloria tiptoed round the issue. "In those relationships, conversation is often not the principal thing. There are other . . ." She struggled to put it gently. At the same time she thought: There's no point in talking about this. Things happen. People go.

Yet wounds have to be licked.

"You mean sex?" asked Paul.

She nodded sadly. "It's very odd. I could never bring myself to . . . to get close to somebody like that." She shuddered. "All that brawn. That thick neck—I take it he has a thick neck—I didn't see his neck outside the supermarket."

"His neck?" mused Paul.

"Yes, I imagine the veins stand out on the side of it, like creepers round the trunk of a tree." She shuddered before continuing. "But listen to me, Paul, you have to put all that behind you. You have to move on."

The advice brought a grimace. "You're not the first person to say that to me. Even my mother's said it—and when your mother tells you to move on . . ."

"I know that's a resounding cliché," Gloria persisted, "and one should never tell somebody to move on, but it's true. The only way you're going to get over this is to . . . well, to move on. Socialise, have fun . . . Invite the whole crowd over to your place. Cook for us, like you used to. Meet new people, even."

"New people?" said Paul. "I like the friends I've got."

"Then get people round," said Gloria. "I'm free next Saturday, for example."

He looked at her. "You and I . . . You weren't suggesting . . ."

He had intended this as a joke, but realised, to his embarrassment, that she was taking it seriously.

"Heavens no," she said, blushing. "All I'm saying is that your old friends are the ones to help you get started on a new life. That may seem paradoxical, but the truth is often paradoxical, you know. I don't know why, but it just is."

When Gloria first discovered Paul, he already had a growing local reputation for his knowledge of food and wine. But had she not coaxed that first book out of him—*Paul Stuart's*

Bordeaux Table—he would probably have remained where she found him: working in the Scottish branch office of a London wine merchant, writing the occasional newspaper column, and from time to time helping friends with their struggling deli business.

"I saw the possibilities," said Gloria. "That's all."

She spotted the potential when she read a small column that Paul occasionally contributed to a local lifestyle magazine. The photograph above the piece helped: "He has an interesting face," she wrote to a colleague. "He's good-looking, but I suspect he doesn't know it—you can always tell. (I can't abide vain men.) The little-boy-lost look helps, and there's something about the way he puts things. It's as if he's taking you into his confidence. People like that: they like the idea that somebody is telling them things that he's not going to tell anybody else, even if they're reading it in a magazine or newspaper."

Gloria worked as a freelance editor, specialising in books that her publishers blandly described as "lifestyle." She had a talent for bringing out the good idea that lurked in sometimes chaotic manuscripts, and at the end producing something coherent. Although most of her work was sent to her by publishers, very occasionally she suggested to them what they might do, in this way crossing the boundary into the territory of the commissioning editor. When she did this, publishers had come to trust her instinct, which more often than not was correct.

"I'm not an agent," she said to Paul. "I'm an editor. It's different. I'm on your side, but not one hundred per cent, if you see what I mean."

"It means you can tell me what to do," said Paul.

Gloria laughed. "I'd never do that. No, it's more a case of telling you that you can't do what you want to do."

"I see."

"But telling you in such a way that you don't think I'm telling you what not to do."

"Right."

"In other words . . . look, you know how it works, don't you?"

He did. And he was grateful to Gloria, not that he tended to express his gratitude very often. She knew, he thought; Gloria knew that he liked her and was grateful. You don't have to spell everything out.

When *Paul Stuart's Bordeaux Table* was published, there was no real reason for it to stand out in its discouragingly crowded field. Food writers, it seemed, were two a penny, with every regional cuisine having been thoroughly covered from all conceivable angles. Julia Child and Elizabeth David had been the trailblazers; those who followed were precisely that: followers. Yet there was something about Paul's writing that gave it particular appeal—and this was picked up by reviewers.

Once it had been described as "insanely readable" by the gushing food editor of a major London paper, the die was cast. There were interviews and television appearances, and on television Paul simply *worked*. In an age of self-promotion, people responded well to his good manners. There was nothing of the diva about him, none of the braggadocio of other well-known chefs. He was, in a word, likeable.

"Okay, Paul," counselled Gloria. "Big success—well done. But . . ." She had had this conversation with so many authors, and the *but* had often proved prophetic. "A first book can be a last book only too easily. The second is the real test. Put everything you have into that."

Paul heeded her advice. The success of the Bordeaux book had emboldened him to resign from his job with the wine merchant, and so he needed the advance that the publishers for whom Gloria worked offered for *Paul Stuart's Provençal Table*. Again, the formula worked, and three months in Provence resulted in a book that was even more enthusiastically received. There then followed a further three French books, one on the food and wines of Portugal, and three on Spanish regions.

By his thirty-sixth birthday, which was when Becky ran off with the personal trainer, Paul had embarked on his tenth book, which was to be *Paul Stuart's Tuscan Table*. By now the success of the enterprise meant that he could employ a part-time researcher to undertake much of the preparatory work, collating the facts that Paul would then seamlessly weave into his conversational narrative. If he wrote knowledgeably— and effortlessly—about *trésors de cuisine* such as a means of preserving meat glaze, it was because his assistant had ferreted out a copy of Mique Grandchamp's *Le cuisinier à la bonne franquette,* published in 1884, and discovered just how one might heat a slightly depleted bottle of Madeira in a pan of hot water, pour in the meat glaze, and then recork the bottle. Similarly, Paul himself would not have had the time to extract the recipe for *Soupe au Pistou* from Eugène Blanchard's *Mets de Provence,* but his assistant had. Every recipe, though, and every wine, was tried and understood before Paul wrote about it; Gloria knew that and knew that she could rely on him.

"Italy next," she said when they met for lunch one day. "What about Tuscany? I know it's the obvious choice, but there's nowhere to beat it. At least not in my view. Cypress trees along ridges, as in a Renaissance painting. Dusty roads. Abbeys tucked away in the folds of hills. Bean stew . . ."

Paul nodded. "All right," he said.

She looked at him. There was a lack of enthusiasm in his tone that she had not heard before. "You don't want to do another Spanish book, do you? I thought you said you wanted something different."

He shrugged. He was not looking at her directly, but seemed to be gazing out of the window. "Tuscany's fine. It'll do."

She looked at him again. "Is something troubling you?"

This brought a further shrug. And then he laid down his knife and fork with the air of one with something to announce.

Plaintively, he told her what had happened. "Becky's gone off with her personal trainer."

For a while Gloria stared at Paul blankly, not saying anything. *At last,* she thought. *At long last.*

Now Paul broke the silence. "You were never too keen on her, were you?" He spoke in a matter-of-fact tone; he did not sound accusing.

Gloria blushed. Her distaste for Becky's selfishness would have to be put carefully. "I just thought that the two of you were rather different people."

Paul took time to weigh this. "Maybe," he said. "I obviously didn't do it for her. I tried, you know."

"I'm sure you did." Gloria thought of Somerset Maugham's *Painted Veil*. It was the classic theme: good man, worthless woman—and, of course, the other way round, the moral failure reversed.

"I did my best to make it work," he sighed. "But I suppose

she'd just had enough. You can't blame somebody for that, can you?"

"No," she said, although without conviction. "Some relationships work—others don't. It's as simple as that."

"I suppose so, but still . . ."

"You needn't reproach yourself."

She found her dislike for Becky growing, now that she could admit it to herself. Paul was everything most women would ever want: he was good-looking, personable, kind, amusing; Becky had obviously failed to appreciate any of this. The personal trainer was exactly the sort of person whom somebody like Becky might fall for, at least in the short term.

Would it last? Gloria was not sure that purely physical attraction could keep a relationship going for long. Personal trainers, like the rest of humanity, lost condition, put on weight, lost their vigour. That was undoubtedly true, but then it was possible that Becky had found a soul-mate, and that the outsider's view of the relationship was all wrong. Perhaps they were simply compatible. Perhaps each had found that the other saw the world in the same way. Perhaps they had just fallen in love, which is not always a matter that can be attributed to looks or sex or some shared enthusiasm. That might even have been the trouble with Paul and Becky—they had never actually loved one another—for all of those four years together. That sort of thing happened; the inertia that for years keeps people doing jobs they do not like, or living in houses they feel uncomfortable in, can keep them in relationships with those they do not love, or sometimes do not even like.

But something else was beginning to worry Gloria. She had experience of writers who suddenly lost their way when their personal lives became unstable. Paul made money for his publishers and that effectively paid a large part, if not all, of her salary. Gloria was far from selfish: her first concern was Paul's welfare, but there were other things at stake here too. A disaster for Paul would be painful for quite a number of others. More was at stake here than Paul's personal happiness.

Gloria saw Paul for a catch-up lunch every month. Now she decided that she would increase the frequency of these meetings, at least until the Tuscan book was safely in production.

"I'm always here for you, Paul," she said at one such lunch, which took place a couple of weeks later. "I know how you must be feeling."

He looked at her doubtfully. Gloria was kind—he had always known that—but had she ever been rejected by anybody? There had never been any mention of boyfriends; she had never said anything about an unhappy love affair in her past. And if you had never experienced that, would you really understand?

He looked at her doubtfully. "Do you?"

"Yes, as it happens I do." She paused. "There are few things worse than the thought that the person with whom you live no longer wants to be in your company. I know that."

"Sorry," said Paul. "I'm sure you do." He sighed. "I know I have to try to get over her."

"Then you must."

"It's just that I keep thinking of her. I miss her. I wake up in the morning and I imagine she's there. But then I turn round and I'm by myself. Corny, isn't it?"

"No, not in the slightest bit corny. Not in the slightest." She reached out to take his hand. It was not how things usually were between them; they never touched. He looked down at her hand, almost with surprise. He gave it a squeeze, and then withdrew his hand from hers, not abruptly, but gently, and slowly. She glanced down, but then looked up again, as if she had surprised herself with the gesture.

"Make an effort," she said. "Think of other things." She paused. "You were going to invite people over. We're waiting, you know."

He smiled at her weakly.

This is potentially very bad, she thought. And the solution that she would most have liked was not, it seemed, remotely possible.

She helped him plan the evening.

"Only old friends," he said.

"Agreed."

"And not too many people. Eight?"

"Ten."

He conceded. "The usual crowd? Jenny and Bill? Bob? Fran? And I can sit next to you?"

She reassured him. "Of course you can. And Fran on the other side, and Jock beside her."

He looked away. "I haven't really got the heart for this, you know. Somehow I feel just . . . just fed up with everything."

"Which is precisely why you need to do something about it." She wanted to shake him, and for a moment her impatience showed.

He looked taken aback. "You're cross with me?"

She swallowed hard. "No . . . well, yes. Yes, I am. You have everything going for you—everything. People like you. They like your books. They buy them. They write to you. You have this nice flat. You've got enough money to live comfortably. You're not at all bad-looking. So why . . ." She stopped. She knew that there was no point: misery was nothing to do with objective good fortune. Misery was like bad weather; it was just there, and no number of optimistic comments could make the weather better.

But for some reason her words had resonated with him. He closed his eyes briefly, as if summoning up resolve, and then nodded. "You're right. Everything you say is right."

She was unprepared for this. "Really? Do you mean . . ."

"I mean that I need to do exactly as you say. I need to stop thinking of Becky. I need to look . . ."

"Forward?"

"Yes, forward."

"Well, I must say that I'm relieved. I thought we were losing you, you know. I thought you were . . . sinking, so to speak."

"Well, I won't. I won't sink."

"Good."

He looked at her, clearly waiting for her to say something more.

"So . . ." She trailed off.

"Yes?"

"So you have this party. You get everybody together. It'll be a sort of announcement that you're starting again. The beginning of the post-Becky era."

"And then?"

She saw her chance. "And then you get back to work on your Tuscany book. It's already six weeks late." She did not mention that the food photographer was waiting for his instructions and had already threatened to cancel.

"I'm sorry."

She was quick to reassure him. "No great disaster. You can

catch up. I suggest that you go to Italy. Finish it there. Do some on-the-ground research."

He looked thoughtful. "Next month. July?"

"Perfect."

"It'll have to be organised. Reservations made and so on—"

She cut him short. "I'll do all of that. I'll book you into that place you told me about, that hotel in Mont-something."

"Montalcino."

"Yes. And I'll arrange the flights, car hire, and so on. Everything. You needn't lift a finger."

He was caught up in her enthusiasm. "It's best to fly to Pisa. I can pick up a car there and drive down. It's only a few hours."

"There you are. Simplicity itself."

"And I'll finish the manuscript. I've only got five or six chapters to go. I've been sitting on them."

"I know." For a moment she imagined all the authors who were sitting on chapters—the piles of paper neatly stacked on their chairs, with the authors sitting on top of them, slightly uncomfortable, and certainly feeling guilty. She smiled at the thought.

"What's so funny?"

Gloria shook her head. "A ridiculous thought. Authors sitting on their chapters."

Paul was earnest. "But you'll get them. I'll deliver."

"I know that too."

He turned his attention to the dinner. "What am I going to give them? I haven't thought about it."

"You decide. You're the famous cookery writer. I'll do the inviting for you—but the food and so on is up to you."

He suggested duck, as it was the first thing that came to mind, and she agreed. "And we'll have Brunello di Montalcino. It's probably the best Italian wine there is. It's my favourite, as it happens."

"My mouth is watering," said Gloria.

*S*he knew all the guests—her circle intersected with Paul's, and she had encountered all of them socially before this.

"His confidence has taken a real battering," she explained when she telephoned with the invitation. "This is his putting a toe back into the water. Gingerly. But we'll need to be careful. We need to keep things upbeat. So no mention of Becky . . . or of unfaithfulness in general. Keep it positive."

Everybody had been understanding, and had assured Gloria that not a single gloomy observation would come from them. "You want Polyanna?" said one of the friends. "You'll get Polyanna in spades!"

When they arrived, the bonhomie was tangible. *Don't overdo it,* thought Gloria, as the ten of them stood in the living room, each with a glass of prosecco in hand.

"Paul's going off to Italy," Gloria announced. "Next week, Paul?"

Paul nodded. "Yes. Next Wednesday."

"*Bravo!*" said Fran.

Paul shrugged. "Hardly heroic," he said.

"But to go off all by yourself . . . ," said Fran.

There was a silence.

"To Tuscany," said Gloria quickly. "Montalcino."

This triggered a memory in Bob. "We went there on our honeymoon," he said. "We were in Siena and Florence, but wanted to get away from the crowds. It's a great place for a honeymoon."

This brought a further silence and another discouraging

glance from Gloria. "It's where they make Brunello di Montalcino," she said. And then, looking disapprovingly at the offender, repeated, "Brunello di Montalcino. Paul's going to serve that this evening with his duck à l'orange, aren't you, Paul?"

Paul nodded. "When you're ready," he said, putting his glass down.

"Duck à l'orange!" said Jenny. "I love your cooking, Paul. I shall have to go to the gym after this . . ." Her voice trailed away before she resumed. "I mean, to lose weight . . ."

There was nervous laughter during which Gloria glanced at Paul, who grinned back at her. Seeing his enjoyment of the situation, she relaxed. Now she said the first thing that came to mind.

"Has anybody ever thought about the way in which cats look at the world?"

The laughter died away. "Not recently," said Paul. "Why do you ask?"

She took a sip of wine. "A story I heard about a cat who lived in New York. It makes one think of how cats understand things."

The guests looked at her expectantly.

"Carry on," said Paul.

"These people lived in a building with ten floors. They lived on the third floor—what we'd call the second floor."

"Counting the ground floor as the first floor," said Paul. "Which is entirely logical, after all."

"Yes, the third floor to them. And so the cat was used to going down two flights of stairs to get to the first floor, where there was a window from which it could get out into the garden." Gloria paused. "Then they moved to another apartment block, one that had rather more floors. They now lived on the fourth floor."

"They went up in the world," remarked Paul.

"And so did the cat," said Fran. "Cats like to be socially mobile."

"It wanted to get out," said Gloria. "Once you let cats out, they'll never be content with staying in. So every morning it kept going down two floors, looking for an exit to the garden."

Nobody said anything. Then Paul laughed. "Reasonable enough."

Gloria nodded. "Perhaps. But what it shows is that even if cats remember some facts, they may be unable to apply the knowledge." She looked at the guests.

"Ah!" said Fran.

"But there's more," Gloria continued. "The cat found a window on the second floor—two storeys down, you see—and he leapt onto the sill. He sat there for some time and then jumped out, thinking, of course, that he was on the first floor. He had quite a fall, landing heavily, and painfully, on the sidewalk below."

Jenny, a cat-lover, winced. "He was all right?"

"Quite badly traumatised," said Gloria. "And thereafter he had a real fear of New York sidewalks. He was fine with windows, but sidewalks worried him."

She looked around the table. Paul met her gaze. Slowly a smile spread across his face. "A distinctive view of causation," he muttered.

Gloria returned his smile. "Yes. Very distinctive."

Bob frowned. "So?" he muttered, and then, to his neighbour, "I'm not wild about cats. Faithless creatures. Disloyal."

The silence, dispelled by the stories, returned.

"So much for cats," said Paul. Then, looking round the table, he announced, "Let's talk about elephants."

They stared at him.

"Elephants in the room, that is. Listen everybody: I'd like to say something. Relationships end—it happens. It's nobody's fault and you get over it. I have. I hope that Becky's happy, and I'm sure she will be. And as for me . . . I want you to know that I'm fine. You don't have to worry about me. You don't have to pretend that four years of my life just aren't there. I can take it. I'm just fine. I wasn't, but I am now, and now that I'm going to Italy, I want you all to know that I'm going to have a great time and . . . and, well, I have a feeling, you see, that something rather unusual is going to happen. I just feel it."

This brought a general murmur of relief.

"It's so difficult," whispered Fran to Bob. "It's so difficult not to talk about things you've been asked not to talk about."

"Like personal trainers . . . Have you seen him, by the way?"

"What was she thinking of? To leave somebody like Paul for Mr. Universe, or whatever he's called."

"Tommy."

"Well, there you have it. Tommy Universe. How could she?"

"Let's not be unkind. We don't know him, do we? He's probably got his good points."

"Oh, undoubtedly." And then a pause, followed by, "No, you're probably right. One shouldn't judge people by appearances. But after a while, wouldn't you get a bit . . . a bit bored?"

"Probably. But what about Paul? He's such a catch."

"He'll be caught in Italy. They're already lying in wait for him—the women."

"I hope he doesn't make the same mistake twice. People do."

There was a nod of agreement. "All the time. People go for the wrong person time and time again."

"Oh well . . ."

"Yes, as you say: oh well." A pause. "You know something? I think Paul's right. Something's going to happen in Italy."

"Good or bad?"

"Oh, good."

"Extremely good?"

"Absolutely."

"Because it could be the opposite, couldn't it? Look at Keats, going off to Italy to die. Those fatal shores. What did the Romantic poets die of when they went to Italy? Malaria?"

"Rupert Brooke died of a fly bite, didn't he? Although that was in Greece, rather than Italy—one of the islands, I think. And von Aschenbach succumbed to cholera. He was fictional, of course."

"Fictional deaths can make us cry real tears."

"The allure of Italy is all about beauty—fatal beauty."

"Could be. And yet . . ."

"And yet it beguiles?"

"And yet it beguiles. That's what beauty does—it beguiles."

"So what's going to happen to Paul?"

"He's going to fall in love, I suspect. That's what happens to so many people who go to Italy. They fall in love. With the country. With the people. They find somebody."

"I really want him to fall in love."

"So do I."

"And I really want somebody to fall in love with him."

"D'accordo."

Silence. Paul had brought in an amuse-bouche of whipped parmesan, white and fluffy as a sorbet.

"Divine," said Fran.

At her end of the table, Gloria smiled. Things were looking much better now. She dipped a spoon into the whipped parmesan, and closed her eyes.

2

There Is No Car

Scotland fell away beneath him, a stretch of green pasture, of hills, of swirling mist. Suddenly they were bathed in sunlight; fields of cloud, topped with crenellations of white, now lay beneath them as their plane pointed south. In his window seat he closed his eyes against the glare, imagining for a few moments their destination, as much an idea, a feeling, as a place. He saw a small tower that he had never seen before, a tower of warm red brick with a pattern of holes for doves. Down below, a man was pulling at a bell rope; as the bell rang, the doves launched themselves from their holes in the brick and fluttered skywards.

He opened his eyes and noticed that the passenger in the seat beside him, a man in perhaps his early fifties, dressed in a lightweight linen suit, was looking at him. The man smiled at him, and he returned the smile.

"What takes you to Pisa?" the man asked. His accent revealed him as Italian.

Paul hesitated, unsure as to whether he wanted to strike up a conversation that went beyond the niceties. He had brought with him a book that was just beginning to engage him, and he was looking forward to getting back to it. But the man smiled at him again, and his natural politeness decided the matter.

"*So parlare Italiano,*" he began. "*Sono . . .*"

The man did not allow him to finish. "Ah!" he said, and then, continuing in Italian, "What a pleasure it is for us Italians to discover somebody who speaks our language."

"I'm sure there are many. Such a beautiful language . . ."

"Yes, but what use is a beautiful language spoken just by oneself? It's all very well for the Spaniards, because there are so many Spanish speakers—all over the world. Even Portuguese has Brazil, but we have just us—just Italy—and after a while we get fed up with speaking only to ourselves. We have heard everything there is to say in Italian."

"Surely not . . ."

"I am not entirely serious. A bit serious, perhaps, but not entirely." Turning in his seat, he extended a hand towards Paul. "But I must introduce myself. I am Rossi—Silvio Rossi."

"I'm Paul Stuart."

Silvio loosened his tie. "Stuart is the name of Scottish kings, is it not? Mary Stuart . . ." He made a chopping gesture across his throat. "She was most unfortunate. Queens cannot choose their neighbours, and if they find they have one who has an axe, then it is most regrettable." He sighed, as if the execution of Mary, Queen of Scots, had been a recent outrage.

"It was a long time ago," Paul said.

Silvio raised an eyebrow. "But I am an historian," he said. "What happened in the past remains rather vivid for me and . . ." He paused, and now removed the tie altogether. "That's better. Yes I find that the past has a much bigger shadow than people believe. It's still with us in so many ways. At our side all the time, whispering into our ear."

"Warning us not to repeat our mistakes?"

Silvio smiled. "We repeat some. Others we're sensible

enough to avoid making more than once. But that's not what I was thinking about. What I was thinking about was the way in which the past determines our character, not just as individuals, but as nations. A child who is treated badly grows up damaged. A people who are subjected to bad treatment will bear resentments, will be suspicious. They will be bad allies."

Paul, who had been holding his book, slipped it into the seat pocket in front of him. He had endured worse conversations on flights, including an attempt at religious conversion, a confession of adultery, and detailed advice on the attractions of Panama as a tax shelter. "You're thinking of?"

Silvio waved a hand airily. "Oh, there are many examples. Russia, for one. Russia is a peasant country. It has a past of serfdom that ended only in the nineteenth century. That made for a vast, stubborn, ignorant population—one that was also very resentful. And they are resentful today— particularly of the West."

"I see."

"They view the West in the same light as they viewed their feudal masters. Authority." He paused. "So western politicians who lecture Russians about human rights or their tendency to invade their neighbours will never change them. Not one bit. You're dealing with a particular sort of bear, you see. One with a history. An abused bear with a short temper."

Paul savoured the metaphor. He was right. "And Italy?"

"Well, that's an interesting case. With us, the important thing to remember is that we are very young. We have lots of history, of course, but Italy itself is a teenager. The Risorgimento was really just yesterday, you'll know. It ended in 1871. That's yesterday. And that means that, as a state, we are still very far from maturity. That's why half the population doesn't really believe that the Italian state exists—or, if it does, they feel that they owe it nothing. We're very disloyal to Rome, you know. We look after ourselves—our family, our city—and we don't like paying taxes to Rome."

"Nobody likes taxes."

"Some like them less than others. Take the Greeks. They have a particular aversion to taxes, and this is because they haven't forgotten that they were once part of the Ottoman Empire and they saw no reason to pay taxes to the Ottomans."

"So you're saying that people don't change?"

Silvio sighed. "They don't. Or if they do, it takes a long time. A very long time."

The plane gave a slight jolt as it encountered a pocket of turbulent air. Paul glanced out of the window, and then returned to the conversation. "May I ask you something?" he said. "Is this what you actually do?"

Silvio shook his head. "I'm an economic historian," he replied. "That's something quite different, but it doesn't stop me having views on these more general matters."

"Economic history," muttered Paul.

"A sobering science. That's why I've been in Scotland. I've been at a conference." He paused. "You didn't tell me why you're going to Pisa."

"To taste food and wine," said Paul.

Silvio looked surprised. "So that's what you do?"

"Yes. I write about it."

"There is a great deal to be said about Italian food."

"Yes, I'm discovering that."

Paul reached for his book.

"I mustn't keep you from your reading."

Paul had not intended to be rude. "Forgive me. I was enjoying our conversation."

"But you must read your book, and I have some papers to

attend to." Silvio reached into his pocket. "Let me give you my card. I'm at the University of Pisa. It has all the details there. If you need help while you're in Italy, please get in touch with me. My door is always open."

Paul thanked him and took the card. Professor Silvio Rossi, it appeared, was not only Professor of Economic History at the University of Pisa, but a member of the Italian Academy of Economic Science and a *cavaliere* of the Republic. He slipped the card into the pocket of his jacket and opened his book.

They arrived in Pisa shortly before eleven in the morning. Paul said goodbye to Silvio in the plane, and once again as they were waiting for their luggage at the baggage carousel.

"Don't forget," said Silvio. "You have my card. I am at your disposal while you're in my country."

Paul thanked him. The first of his two suitcases had now been disgorged, and he struggled to retrieve it. A few minutes later the second case appeared, and in that mood of relief and gratitude that always follows a safe reunion with luggage, he began to make his way to the office of the car hire firm with which Gloria had made the reservation of a small saloon car.

And that was the point at which the journey, so smooth until then, began to go badly wrong.

"Your name?" said the reservation clerk.

Paul handed him the booking confirmation Gloria had printed out for him. "It's all there," he said.

The clerk took the piece of paper. There was an air of suspicion in the way in which he held it—as if this might be a forgery of some sort. He looked down at his computer and typed in a few digits. Then he scrutinised the form again, glanced at Paul, and then looked back at his screen.

"I am afraid there is no such reservation," he said.

Paul leaned forward, trying to get a glimpse of the computer screen. The clerk shifted it slightly, to ensure that it was even less visible.

"I'm sorry, *dottore,* but there is nothing. This reservation has been made by one of our overseas offices, and they have not confirmed it with us. This has happened before. It is not our fault."

Paul felt the back of his neck becoming warm. "But it says very clearly . . ."

The clerk cut him short. "There is nothing here on my screen." He gave Paul a look of reproach. "Nothing. There is no car."

"But that print-out . . ." Paul pointed at his piece of paper, now seemingly so much more valuable than before. "That piece of paper has the name of your firm at the top and below that it has the words *Reservation confirmed.* Look. Right here. *Reservation confirmed.*"

The clerk shook his head. "That document is no longer valid."

"What do you mean by that?" challenged Paul. He was being polite, but was unable to prevent a testy note from creeping into his voice.

"I mean that if a document of that type is not confirmed by an entry in the main computer, then it ceases to have any validity. That is the way these things are." It was the voice of the patient bureaucrat, explaining how, by immutable custom, the working world ordered its affairs. But even the strictest system has room for humanity. "However, we have a spare car. It is our very last car in hand; it is a very busy time of year, you'll understand. We can allocate that to you instead of this non-existent car you have been promised."

"For the same rate?" asked Paul.

The clerk looked at him lugubriously, as if disappointed that Paul could even suspect that they would consider a higher rate. "At exactly the same rate," he confirmed. "It is much bigger than the car you claim to have booked . . ."

"That I *did* book," corrected Paul.

"It is bigger than that car," repeated the clerk. "It is a Mercedes-Benz. I can prepare the documents for you."

Paul relaxed. He was not yet in Montalcino, but the prospect of arriving there before dinner was beginning to seem more real. "You're very kind," he said to the clerk.

The clerk bowed his head. Tapping out details on his keyboard, he printed two sheets of paper for Paul to sign before reaching for a set of keys.

"You'll find the car outside," he said, and told him the row in the car park where it would be parked. "Show your copy to the woman at the barrier, and she will let you through."

It was now midday, and the sun was at its zenith. When he left the cool of the car rental office, with its sharp, air-conditioned air, Paul felt it press down on him like a warm hand; it was humid, and his shirt clung to him uncomfortably, the damp patches showing dark through the fabric. He wiped his brow. It would be cooler in Montalcino, several hundred feet higher than Pisa.

He looked about him. The form gave the colour of the car and the registration number, and he started to make his way slowly along the lines of vehicles in the relevant row. By the time he reached the end, he had failed to find it. He looked along the line of vehicles in the neighbouring row; perhaps they had made a mistake and parked it in the wrong place. Slowly he worked his way along that row too, checking the number of each Mercedes-Benz. It was not there—nor was it in the row beyond that. That left only one possible line of cars, and he now checked this carefully, with the same result.

He felt hot and frustrated. He had heard that car hire in Italy could be an arcane, rather trying process, but he had hoped that Gloria's arrangements would somehow avoid any difficulties. Obviously not, he said to himself.

The relatively short time he had spent in the sun was enough to make him thirsty. Looking around, he saw on the far side of the car park, separated from it by only a modest fence, a small café. He would find himself something to drink there—something cool and refreshing—before going back to the car rental office. There must be other car parks, he decided; perhaps an employee had put it in the wrong car park altogether; airports were complicated places, with all their roads and buildings, and that sort of mistake could be made only too easily.

He sat in the café for fifteen minutes or so, enjoying the air-conditioning and the bottle of chilled mineral water he had ordered. Then he returned to the terminal building, where the office of Personal-Drive Italia was located. The clerk for some reason pretended not to recognise him, and solemnly noted down his details afresh.

"So you say the car isn't there," he said once Paul had finished with his story.

"That's so," said Paul. "I have looked very carefully and it isn't there."

The clerk stared at him. "Yet you signed for it."

Paul frowned. "I signed the rental agreement."

The clerk shook his head. "No, you signed for the car itself. Look . . ." He took the form from Paul. "Here—you see—here and here. That says, *I have received the above-mentioned car in good condition.* That is your signature, I take it."

"Of course it is. You were here when I signed it. You gave it to me. You."

The clerk looked away. "Under this agreement," he intoned, "you are liable for the car once it comes into your possession."

"But it never did!" exploded Paul. "I never found the car. I've just tried to tell you that."

"That is not what the document says," retorted the clerk.

For a few moments Paul was speechless. Then he spoke coldly and decisively. "I must speak to the manager," he said. "Please call him."

The clerk's eyes narrowed. "The manager is away."

"Where?"

"He is at the funeral of his mother. In Ravenna."

Paul tried to decide whether this was a lie. It was difficult to tell.

"In that case I want to see the assistant manager," he said.

The clerk replied quickly. "I am the assistant manager."

Paul looked up at the ceiling. "I suggest we forget the whole business, then."

The clerk shrugged. "When are you going to bring the car back? I can't cancel the contract until the car has been returned."

Paul gasped. "I have never seen this car," he said, chiselling out each word for emphasis. "How can I return something I've never had?"

"Then you will be liable for the whole cost of the car."

Paul closed his eyes. "I'm going to call the police," he said.

The clerk shrugged again. "There is a policeman standing over there," he said. "You see him? You can call him if you like."

Paul strode across the arrivals hall and approached the

policeman. The officer was talking to a woman running a small luggage stall, but he broke away when Paul addressed him.

"I am having a bit of trouble over there," said Paul, nodding in the direction of the car rental desk. "I am being falsely accused of taking a car that I have never so much as seen. I believe this is an attempt at extorting money from me."

The policeman adjusted his belt. "I shall accompany you, sir," he said. "Let's see what's going on."

Paul felt relieved that here was somebody who might penetrate the fog of obfuscation into which it seemed he had wandered. But once at the desk, his relief proved to be short-lived.

"This gentleman," said the clerk, rising to greet the policeman, "has disposed of one of our vehicles. He refuses to return it, and I have simply informed him of the consequences."

The policeman frowned, and turned to face Paul. "This is a very serious matter," he said. "Where is this car?"

Paul drew in his breath. "There is no car," he said. "I have never touched it."

This was the signal for the clerk to pass a copy of the rental document to the policeman. "Here is the proof that he took it," he said. "You'll see his signature down at the bottom there. That establishes that he took possession of the car— the same car that he now refuses to hand back."

The policeman studied the piece of paper. "Is this your signature, sir? Is your name . . ." He stumbled over the pronunciation. "Paul Stuart?"

"That's me," said Paul. "And that's my signature too."

"In that case," said the policeman, "you must accompany me to the police station."

"Oh, this is absurd," said Paul, his voice rising markedly.

The policeman reached out to touch him on the arm. "You must control yourself, sir. It doesn't help to shout."

"But I have never even seen this car," Paul protested. "I have had nothing to do with it. Nothing."

The policeman looked at him guardedly. "But you have signed this document."

"I signed it before I went to look for the car," said Paul.

"But that's not what it says here," said the policeman.

Paul glared at the clerk, who simply stared at his screen, as if waiting for a troublesome client to go away so as to allow him to get back to his work. He looked at his watch. If he had to go to the police station he would do it, so that he could get on with the task of finding another car. And at the police station, he imagined that he might find somebody who would be able to take a more intelligent view of the situation than this junior officer.

"I'm ready to accompany you to the police station," Paul said. "Although I shall have to come in your car, as I don't have one myself."

The policeman smiled. "You mustn't make light of these things," he said in a not unfriendly tone. "Car theft is a serious charge, you know."

Paul opened his mouth to say something, but found that he had no words. His Italian, his English, his French all seemed to have deserted him. *Kafka,* he thought, and then, more appropriately he felt, *Lewis Carroll.*

3

I'm So Sorry, *Dottore*

$\mathcal{H}$e was passive as they took his fingerprints, partly because he had no alternative, and partly because he was by that stage in a state of mild shock. He found it hard to believe that this was happening to him: that in Italy, a member state of the European Union, a signatory to conventions on human rights, suddenly and for no reason at all—or no sound reason—one could be taken off in a police car and fingerprinted like a common criminal. And even while he was reflecting on this, worse was in preparation.

"You will be questioned shortly," said the policeman taking his prints. "In the meantime, you will be kept in safety."

He was unprepared for this—"kept in safety" from what?

"But I'm in no danger," he said politely. "Why do I have to be kept in safety?"

The policeman looked scornful. "It's not your safety I'm talking about," he said. "It's the public's."

Paul shook his head in puzzlement. "I'm sorry, *ispettore . . .*"

"Not *ispettore,*" he snapped. "Not yet."

"Sorry, but I just don't follow you. What has the public got to do with this?"

The policeman sighed. When he answered it was as if to explain something very elementary. "We're here to protect the public, right? To protect them from the likes of you." He paused. "Understand?"

Paul could not help but laugh. "From the likes of me? But what have I done to make me a danger to the public?"

The policeman inspected the piece of paper on the desk in front of him. "Car theft," he said.

Paul groaned. "Car theft?"

"That's what I said," repeated the policeman. "We can't let car thieves wander about stealing other people's cars, can we? No, we cannot. So that's why we have to lock you up."

Paul sat quite still. It had been possible until then to treat the whole experience as a ridiculous diversion, even if an irritating one. Now, though, the matter was becoming deadly serious.

"I need a lawyer," he said, as firmly as he could.

"That's what they all say," said the policeman, brushing aside Paul's request. "Lawyers, lawyers, lawyers. All this talk of lawyers. That's the trouble with Italy today—lawyers." He looked at his watch. "I'm sorry, I don't have the time to talk. The *Commissario* himself is coming in a couple of hours. You can talk to him, if you like."

He rose from the desk and stood beside Paul, who was still seated. "This way," he said, gesturing towards the door.

Paul got to his feet. He felt unsteady, and for a brief moment he imagined that he was going to faint. He took a deep breath, and the feeling passed.

"Are you going to come quietly?" asked the policeman.

"Of course," muttered Paul.

"Good," said the policeman. "It's always best to co-operate with the police. Sometimes people don't, and it gets tricky—quite unnecessarily. You know I had to arrest the Prime Minister once? He made a terrific fuss. Swore at us in dialect. Kicked one of my colleagues."

They were making their way through the door when the policeman made this comment.

"The Prime Minister?" asked Paul.

"Yes," said the policeman. "Not the current one, of course, but a previous one—some time ago. We often arrest our prime ministers in Italy. You must know that—if you read the papers."

"For car theft?" asked Paul.

The policeman remained impassive. "Not that," he said. "For all sorts of other things."

"You'll be arresting the Pope next," said Paul. "Ever done that?"

The policeman shook his head. "No jurisdiction. The Pope technically doesn't live in Italy at all. The Vatican isn't part of our national territory."

"I see."

"But of course if the Holy Father asked us in to arrest somebody, we'd do it—in a spirit of co-operation, you see."

"Naturally. It's good to co-operate. And the more people you can arrest, the better, I suppose."

This remark was greeted with approval. "Exactly," said the policeman. "And I must say that I'm terribly sorry to be arresting somebody as obviously reasonable as yourself. I hope you don't get more than a year or two."

They had reached the end of a corridor, and were standing outside a grey door with a round observation window—a peephole—at eye level.

"On the subject of the Prime Minister," said the policeman, as he extracted a key from his pocket, "of course he was innocent. Being arrested just went with the job, I suppose." He paused. "Do they ever arrest the Prime Minister back where you come from?"

"Very rarely," said Paul.

"Too clever?" asked the policeman.

"Possibly."

"He'll make a slip one of these days, no doubt. They always do. Then they'll get him."

Paul looked about him. At the end of the corridor was a window through which he could see the sky. This was the same Tuscan sky under which he had planned to sit and write. How long would it be, he wondered, before he saw it again?

"I regret to say that you're going to have to share," said the policeman as he turned the key in the lock. He leaned forward to whisper to Paul. "This fellow inside—we've been looking for him for some time. Multiple thefts—with violence. Suspected of practically everything." He shook his head. "Nasty. He's called Calogero Occhidilupo, would you believe it? These southern names! Salvatore, Pasquale, Valentinianu, and so on. Then they go and add it to some really strange family name like Occhidilupo—wolf eyes, literally, just like the pasta. What are they thinking of, I ask myself?"

The door opened. Nervously peering over his custodian's shoulder, Paul caught a glimpse of his cellmate. He recoiled.

"Listen," he whispered to the policeman. "You can't put me in there with a man like that."

The policeman shook his head. "We're very short of space," he said. "And you should have thought of this before you stole that car."

"I have never stolen a car," said Paul. "Never."

Now he thought quickly. Reaching into his pocket, he took out the card given him by his companion on the plane. "Can you do one thing for me?" he asked the policeman.

"One small favour? Could you phone this man and tell him I'm here—that's all."

The policeman examined the card. "Professore Silvio Rossi," he read out loud. Then, looking at Paul, he asked, "You know the *Cavaliere*?"

"He's a very close friend," said Paul. That was technically true, he thought: we did sit together in a crowded economy compartment of a plane; that surely made us close friends.

The policemen hesitated. "I suppose there's no harm . . ."

"None at all," said Paul. "In fact, I'm sure the *Cavaliere* would be very grateful to you. And, who knows? He might even mention your helpfulness to somebody . . ." He pointed up at the ceiling. "Somebody higher up."

The policeman smiled. "I'll be happy to make this call," he said.

Paul heaved a sigh of relief. "Straightaway?" he asked.

"*Immediatamente.*"

The policeman stood aside to allow Paul to enter the cell. "I'll be back shortly to check that our southern friend is behaving himself," he said, nodding towards the figure seated on one of the cots.

Paul took a step forward as the door closed behind him. Hardly daring to look directly at the other man, he crossed the cell to the other cot and sat down. Then, glancing quickly at his companion, he started to utter a greeting. His voice trailed away as he took in his cellmate's appearance.

Occhidilupo was a man in his forties with the wiry look of the hardened mountain shepherd. His head was small—too small even for his slight body—and his brow virtually non-existent. A ridge of eyebrows was topped only by the smallest ledge until it reached a thick mane of dark hair, roughly swept backwards. Although he had no moustache or beard, the rest of his face, including his nose, was covered with dark hair.

Paul's eyes fell to the hands. These were folded on his lap and were also covered with a thick growth of hair. The nails, which were long and uncut, looked remarkably like claws.

Paul tried once more to speak. *"Ciao,"* he said, his voice sounding tense and strangled.

Occhidilupo's eyes flashed as he gave his reply—a sound that Paul had difficulty interpreting but that sounded very much like a growl.

Paul raised a hand in what he hoped was a friendly gesture. "So . . . ," he began.

Occhidilupo was watching him.

"So," Paul continued. "So here we are."

Occhidilupo growled again. This time, though, it sounded more like a snarl.

Paul looked at his feet.

Suddenly Occhidilupo spoke. "What they get you for, huh?"

Paul shook his head sadly. He would need to be imaginative. *"Omicidio eccezionale,"* he said. He was not sure whether such an offence, exceptional homicide, existed, but it certainly sounded more serious—and frightening, he hoped—than the mere *suspicion of everything* for which Occhidilupo had been arrested.

He had made the right choice. A look of admiration—fleeting, admittedly, but there nonetheless—had crossed the other man's face. "How many, huh?" he asked.

Paul thought quickly. One should not be too boastful. "How many bodies?" he asked. "Seven. Or at least those are the ones they're charging me with." Then he added, "Huh."

Occhidilupo's eyes widened. This, Paul thought, was a

good sign, and precisely the effect that he had sought to create. If Occhidilupo were impressed, then that would mean
that he would be unlikely to start anything.

Now Paul decided to affect a yawn. "I'm dead tired," he
said. "I need to get some rest." He paused before continuing,
"It was a long chase, you see."

Occhidilupo said nothing as Paul lay down on the grubby
blanket of his cot. From his prone position, he was able to
watch—from under half-closed eyelids—the other man. He
was staring at him, the eyes reflecting the weak glow from
the small ceiling light. He was not moving, though, which
afforded Paul some measure of reassurance. And he was
tired, after all the stress he had experienced, and his eyelids
were becoming increasingly heavy. He struggled to keep
awake, but his eyes now closed completely and there was a
distant buzzing sound in his head, like the sound of bees in
summer.

*D*ottore!"

The voice broke through his dream—a confused, strange
narrative in which he was pursuing Becky down a colonnade,
being jeered at in Italian by small, lively boys.

"*Dottore!*"

He opened his eyes. The policeman who had admitted
him to the cell was bending over him, his hand shaking his
shoulder. Behind him stood Silvio Rossi, peering at him with
palpable anxiety.

Paul sat up sharply, trying to make sense, in his confusion,
of his whereabouts.

"My dear friend," said the Professor. "What a terrible
occurrence."

Paul rose to his feet, rubbing the sleep from his eyes.

"The *Cavaliere* will take care of you now," said the policeman. "I telephoned him immediately."

"You have been of great assistance," said the Professor to the policeman, glancing as he spoke at Occhidilupo on the other side of the cell. "My friend the *Commissario* will hear of your helpfulness."

The policeman gestured towards the door. "There's no need to linger here," he said. "We can complete the paperwork once we're outside. The official discharge, you see . . ."

They left the cell, the policeman locking the door behind him. A short way down the corridor there was a small, well-lit office, and they were now led into this and invited, with elaborate politeness, to sit down.

"All I need is a signature," said the policeman, pointing to a form on the desk. "This is merely to confirm that you have been unharmed during your . . . your unfortunate spell in police custody."

"It has been a major mistake," said the Professor.

"We're very sorry," said the policeman. "I have already sent somebody to arrest that man in the car rental office. He's probably already in custody."

"Good," said the Professor.

Paul took the pen proffered him and signed the form.

"That concludes the whole affair," said the policeman. "And may I repeat, *Cavaliere*, how much we regret this administrative error."

The Professor nodded. "We shall speak no more of it," he said.

Outside, the Professor led Paul to a smart grey car parked beside a number of police vehicles. "We can have a coffee at a place I know near here," he said. "You can tell me how it all happened."

They parked and went into a roadside café. A waiter, who greeted the Professor as *Cavaliere,* took their order and appeared almost immediately thereafter with steaming cups of milky coffee. Paul sipped his appreciatively and began his account of events. When he finished, the Professor shook his head in astonishment. "Most, most unfortunate," he said. "But the important thing is that you are now free to proceed with your trip."

"Thanks to you."

The Professor waved a careless hand. "My role was very small. A single telephone call to my good friend the *Questore.* That was all. I simply told him that I could vouch for you and that you couldn't possibly have stolen a car because you were with me on the plane and you would not have had the time. He accepted everything."

"Thank you. I'm extremely grateful."

"It was nothing. But, look, what are your plans now? Will you be leaving directly for Montalcino?"

"If I can find a car to rent," said Paul. "I'll need one there— it's off the beaten track."

"Of course," said the Professor.

"Perhaps I could try another car rental place," said Paul. "I assume there are others."

The Professor frowned. "You know what the problem is?" he said. "It's a holiday weekend. That's why all the rental cars are out."

"So I won't find anything?"

The Professor scratched his head. "I fear that you won't find one through any of the main companies, but I have a contact, as it happens."

Paul was hardly surprised. He knew about Italian networks, about their insidious ubiquity and their power. To be a *cavaliere* of the Republic, one would be bound to have a particularly good network, and that seemed to be the case with Silvio Rossi.

"There's somebody I know who rents out commercial vehicles," continued the Professor. "That's his business, you see. He may well have a small van or something like that."

"I'm not fussy," said Paul. "Anything that's capable of getting from A to B."

The Professor laughed. "From A to B? Well, that demonstrates great flexibility on your part." He finished his coffee. "Shall we go? I can take you right there."

In the car on the way, the Professor raised the subject of Paul's cellmate.

"They should never have put you in with a man like that," said the Professor, disapprovingly. "I'll raise the issue with the *Commissario,* and possibly with the *Questore* himself."

Paul was keen to make little of it. He had already caused his friend enough inconvenience and was unwilling to add to it.

"Please don't," he said. "It was no hardship."

"Did you speak to him?" asked the Professor.

"A few words," said Paul. "He wanted to know why I had been arrested. Not much more than that."

The Professor nodded. "Did you notice his forehead?" he asked.

"Yes. It was a bit . . . recessive."

The Professor laughed. "That's putting it mildly. And his hands—all that hair on the top of his hands. Did you see that?"

"Yes, I suppose I did."

"Did you get his name?" asked the Professor. "Something southern, I suspect."

"He was called Occhidilupo," said Paul. "Calogero Occhidilupo."

The Professor let out a whoop of laughter. "Perfect!" he exclaimed. And then, half-turning to Paul, he asked, "Have you heard of Cesare Lombroso by any chance?"

The name sounded vaguely familiar, but Paul shook his head.

"Lombroso was a very great Italian criminologist," said the Professor. "He published his major works in the nineteenth century. He was very interested in criminal types."

Paul listened attentively.

"He believed that criminality was reflected in the physical features," said the Professor. "He illustrated this with beautiful sketches of the heads and faces of various scoundrels. Typical Sicilan murderer, Neapolitan thief, Puglian degenerate, and so on. They all looked the part, with their scowling expressions and close-set eyes. Lombroso could take one look at them and predict what sort of crimes they were likely to commit."

Paul said nothing.

"That Occhidilupo of yours," went on the Professor. "He was a good illustration of the proposition that Lombroso was right. You could hardly mistake him for a choirboy, could you?"

"I suppose not," said Paul.

"I'd be very interested to see his brain," said the Professor. "In a specimen jar, of course. One wouldn't want to get too close to somebody like that when he still had his brain *in situ*, so to speak."

"Biological determinism," observed Paul.

"Nothing wrong with that," said the Professor. "Lombroso was fundamentally right: had DNA been known about in his day, he would merely have put it all down to the individual genome. Some people just have a bad genome, you see."

"Possibly."

"No, definitely," said the Professor. "The problem these days is that people just don't see the obvious—or they see it, but won't admit it. Of course our faces reveal our character—of course they do."

Paul was thinking of Becky. He had once heard her face described as vain and had been outraged. But was it?

"Well?" asked the Professor.

"Possibly," said Paul. "I suppose that if emotions register on the face . . ."

"Which of course they do," said the Professor. "Anger shows, doesn't it? Resentment? Naturally. Benevolence? Again, yes. So why not malevolence, guilt, deception—all those vices?"

"Well, those may be passing states . . . and perhaps the head, the face, or whatever doesn't *create* the attitude so much as *reflect* it." Yes, he thought; that was the flaw in the Lombrosan position.

But Silvio Rossi was not impressed by this logic. "Pah!" he said. "Anyway, here we are. This is the turning that leads to my friend's place."

The headquarters of Central Commercial Vehicle Hire occupied a fenced compound at the end of a dusty side street. The office was in a temporary building near the gate—not much more than a shed—and it was here that they found the owner, a squat, slightly overweight man in a shiny blue suit. As they entered, he sprang to his feet and pumped the Professor's hand in an enthusiastic handshake.

"*Cavaliere*, what an honour!"

The Professor acknowledged the greeting and proceeded to introduce him to Paul. "This is Claudio," he said. "He is a very helpful person."

Claudio beamed at the compliment. "I do my best," he said.

"You do very well, *ingenere*," said the Professor, using the courtesy title of *engineer*. "My friend here is in need of a car for a few weeks. He is not too fussy about what sort. We're not looking for a Maserati."

Claudio laughed, and then his face fell. "Alas, all my cars are out," he said. "The holiday weekend, you know . . ."

"No vans?"

Claudio shook his head. "All rented out for the next month to a contractor from Grosseto, I'm afraid." He looked apologetically at Paul. "I'm so sorry, *dottore* . . ."

The Professor looked dejected. "Well, I suppose it can't be helped."

But it seemed that Claudio had had an idea. "I could give you another vehicle," he said, "rather than send you away empty-handed."

The Professor brightened. "There you are, Claudio— I knew you wouldn't let me down."

"For you, *Cavaliere*, nothing would be too much trouble." He turned to Paul. "It is the last vehicle I have available. It will be a bit slow, but it will get you to where you want to go."

"Very satisfactory," said the Professor. "What is it, Claudio?"

Claudio looked slightly embarrassed. "It's a bulldozer, *Cavaliere*." And then he added, "A very reliable one, you understand." He smiled at Paul. "This bulldozer will give you no trouble at all, *dottore*—I promise you that."

4

Are You Sure You're Not from Rome?

$\mathcal{D}$riving his newly rented bulldozer slowly down the road south, Paul reflected on the curious events of the previous day. It was a promising morning—the heat that one would normally expect in July was ameliorated by the arrival overnight of cool breezes from the north; now, at eight in the morning, the temperature was comfortable and the wide-open windows of the bulldozer would ensure against any build-up of heat. He had spent the night at the Professor's house in a leafy suburb of Pisa, the bulldozer parked outside the front gate and providing a strong talking point for the neighbours.

Paul and the Professor's wife, Antonietta, had established an immediate rapport, strengthened when Paul had offered to cook the evening meal with her. Afterwards the three of them had sat in the drawing room and enjoyed an amiable conversation until Paul's tiredness showed.

"You must get some sleep now," the Professor had said. "You have had an exhausting day. Sleep deprivation, you know, is a major cause of anti-social behaviour—and accidents too. Look at all the big accidents—the spectacular ones—and you'll find that those involved were sleep-deprived."

"You would not wish to have an accident with a bulldozer," said Antonietta. "You could easily slice another car in half with the blade. *Disastro!*"

"You remember that big explosion at Chernobyl?" said the Professor. "All the people in the control room were sleepy—they had just changed from day to night shifts. And that tanker that ran aground in Alaska . . ."

Antonietta raised a hand. "Poor Paolo is very tired, my dear. We can talk about sleep deprivation some other time."

Paul had sensed the onset of another of the Professor's enthusiasms, and was relieved that the evening was drawing to a close. He slept well, dreamlessly he thought, and the following morning left shortly after breakfast, waved down the road by his hosts and by a small crowd of animated neighbours who had emerged from their houses to witness his departure.

He had been shown how to operate the bulldozer the previous afternoon. At first, when Claudio led them out into the yard to inspect it, he had imagined that he was joking. Yet this was Italy, and it seemed that unlikely—even surreal—things could happen here at any moment. When, all those years ago, he had been a student in Florence, he had sensed that this was a society under the surface of which there lurked strange goings-on, but protected by the self-absorption of youth, he had never bothered to find out what they were. Now, with the awareness of one in his late thirties, he was beginning to see.

Claudio had quickly made it clear that he was entirely serious, and the Professor was too.

"Don't be put off by the fact that it's a bulldozer," said the Professor. "Our human categories are often far too exclusive, too limiting. We need to open them up to allow us to seize opportunities."

Claudio nodded sagely. "The *Cavaliere* is quite right," he said. "As ever." He tapped the bulldozer in a proprietary manner and began to explain how the machine worked.

"You'll notice," he said, "that this is a tracked bulldozer. Some of them can be very clumsy machines, but this has special lightweight tracks that are suitable for use on the road. They're not much different from wheels, actually. It's fine on the road—just like a big truck."

"That's right," said the Professor. "You can drive this one on the road without any difficulty. I wouldn't hesitate to do so myself."

Claudio led them to the side, where a step on the bulldozer bodywork enabled the driver to get into the cabin. "If you follow me up here," he said, "I can show you the controls."

The ignition was demonstrated, as were the five forward and two reverse gears. "The second reverse gear is to enable you to get out of trouble quickly," said Claudio. "If you create a landslip, for example, you may need to go backwards very fast." He paused, and smiled at Paul. "Not that you'll be doing that. You see, I don't think you'll need to operate the blade."

"No," said Paul. "I wasn't planning to."

"But I'll show you how it works, anyway," said Claudio. "You never know."

"No, you don't," said the Professor. He had now joined them and was hanging on to the outside of the cab, peering in through the window.

Claudio pointed to a prominent lever. "You pull that towards you to raise the blade—the normal position for travelling—and then you push it away from you to lower it. Simple."

"Could you show us, Claudio?" asked the Professor.

"*Volentieri, Cavaliere,*" said Claudio. "I shall have to start the engine, though." He turned to Paul, wagging a finger to emphasise his point. "Never operate the blade when the engine is turned off—you'll drain the battery very quickly if you do that. The hydraulic system takes a lot of battery power. Understand?"

Paul nodded. He was wondering how he could get out of this. It was an utterly ridiculous situation to find oneself in—to be about to rent a bulldozer, of all things, and then to drive it off along roads that were challenging enough for a foreign driver, even for one in an ordinary car. He could simply decline, of course, but he sensed that this would be difficult to do. The Professor had been inordinately kind to him, and to refuse now would surely be considered bad manners; and yet they had no right to force him into what was, after all, a commercial contract. No, he would have to be strong. He would have to say how much he appreciated their help, but that he had decided to make his way to Montalcino by bus and then simply to walk once he was there. That was an entirely rational plan, and yet, and yet . . . were these people, charming though they might be, entirely rational?

They dismounted.

"So," said the Professor. "That's everything fixed up. What a relief it must be."

"I'm . . . ," began Paul.

The Professor reached out to touch his arm. "Please, Mr. Stuart, there is no need to express your gratitude. Claudio and I are only too pleased to help a visitor to our country—especially one who can use our language so well."

"Indeed," said Claudio. "Whatever we can do to help, we shall do. So shall we go and sign the rental agreement? It's

pretty straightforward—you take it by the week on a renewable basis. How long do you wish to be in . . ."

"Montalcino," supplied the Professor.

Claudio's face broke into a broad smile. "Ah, Montalcino!
Now that's a very pleasant place to be. I went there once or
twice when I was a young man. I knew somebody who lived
down in the Val d'Orcia, and we cycled up to Montalcino
from below—quite a ride it was."

"One of those roads that never seems to get to the top,"
remarked the Professor. "Of which there are many in this
life, alas."

"Hah! Very well put, *Cavaliere*," said Claudio. "In those
days, Montalcino was a rather forgotten small town—not
much more than a village. There was a piazza, I remember, where they had some sort of municipal fountain. Small
boys stood around throwing stones at the fish until a woman
came out of one of the houses and chased them away with
a broom. Isn't it strange how some memories linger?" He
paused, lost in the recollection. Then he continued, "So how
long will you be up there, *dottore*?"

Paul did not answer for a moment. He sensed that he was
at one of those crossroads when a decision would somehow
affect the shape of the rest of his life. He would have to say
no; there was no other possibility. He could not drive off in
a bulldozer. He could not subject himself to the amazement
and ridicule of other road users as he trundled through the
Italian countryside in this large steel-bladed vehicle. It was
simply inconceivable.

"Three weeks," he said.

It was his voice that spoke. It was he who had said it. And
yet it was not what he had intended.

"That's fine," said Claudio. "I have somebody wanting to rent this in September, but that gives us plenty of time." He smiled encouragingly. "So, are you happy to sign a rental agreement for three weeks, renewable, of course, if you want a few extra days? All you'd have to do is phone to extend the period."

"Yes," said Paul.

He could hardly believe that he had said it, and for a few moments the thought crossed his mind that he was acting in a state of dissociation. He had read about that recently—about how, when tired or stressed, we might act without having any real control over our actions. And the things we might do in a state of dissociation might be bizarre, be out of character—just as this was.

"Good," said the Professor. "After you've signed, you can bring it round to my place. We'll put you up for the night, as you can't go off this late in the afternoon."

"I wouldn't drive it at night," warned Claudio. "It has headlights, of course, but at night one might just misjudge things and the blade could hit something—heaven forfend, of course."

The Professor laughed. "At least you have Saint Christopher on your side. Did you see the large medallion in the cab?"

Paul said that he had.

"Of course he's the patron saint for all travellers, whatever their mode of transport," mused the Professor. "Although there's always Saint Joseph of Copertino. He's the patron saint of air travellers because he was famous for having levitated."

"In the air?" asked Claudio. "He went up in the air?"

"Yes," said the Professor. "He levitated and then travelled

quite considerable distances, going sideways through the air. Remarkable."

"Italy is full of surprises," said Claudio.

"Mind you," continued the Professor, "the patron saint of bulldozers must surely be Saint Benedict of Nursia, who looks after those involved in construction."

"If you say so, *Cavaliere,*" agreed Claudio.

They walked back to the office, where Paul signed the contract, handed over his credit card to pay, and closed his eyes briefly in acceptance of fate. Saint Benedict of Nursia, he said to himself, will you let me get away with this? Not that he believed in the power of saints to intervene in our affairs; and even then Saint Benedict was probably the wrong saint anyway. Was there a patron state for those embarking on pure folly?

He turned to the Professor. "Forgive me for asking, *professore*—is there a patron saint for fools?"

The Professor did not hesitate. "Saint Simeon," he said. "He was known as the Holy Fool. He behaved in a very foolish way . . ."

Like me, thought Paul.

". . . and all the time he was secretly performing acts of great kindness."

"I see."

"So he is now the patron saint of fools of all sorts," concluded the Professor.

Including those who hire bulldozers, thought Paul.

The Professor was looking at him in a bemused way. "I hope you're not thinking yourself foolish?"

"Well . . ."

"Because you are not being at all unwise." He paused as he

put a brotherly arm around Paul's shoulder. "Listen, *dottore,* in Italy we are always open to new experiences. We are not like our dear friends the Germans—they are always so careful and so measured; we are not. We like to live. We like to throw caution to the winds. We delight in life. Going off to Montalcino on a bulldozer may seem odd, even foolish, but it is not. It will get you there, and once there it will take you to other places you may wish to visit. So embrace the opportunity. Set off with a song in your heart. You have a bulldozer; you have an empty road ahead of you; you have three weeks of freedom in the most beautiful landscape in Europe. Is that foolishness? Is it really? I think not, *dottore*—I think not."

Now, sitting in the cab of the bulldozer as it trundled along a quiet side road, Paul could enjoy the view that his elevated position afforded him. It had been a surprise to him to discover just how commanding that view was: as cars passed him, he saw only their tops; as he approached a corner, he was able to see around and beyond it; as he drove past walls, he saw into the farmyards or gardens beyond. A couple lying on a lawn in intimate embrace looked up to see Paul waving to them as he went past; a man pruning an apple tree near the roadside, high on his ladder, finding himself eye to eye with Paul as the bulldozer growled by, was able only to open his mouth in surprise. And beyond such unexpected human encounters, there stretched the Tuscan countryside, now plains sloping down to the coast, now rolling hills blue in the distance under the first shimmering of heat haze.

The bulldozer's slow pace meant that a line of cars would build up behind it, but Paul, being able to see very clearly what was coming, could wave people past when it was safe for them to overtake. They signalled their appreciation by sounding their horns, pleased at the courtesy of this construction worker, bound, they assumed, for some pressing local task of earthmoving but still considerate of those with longer distances to cover. A police car went past, slowed down momentarily, but then sped off again. Nobody imagined that the bulldozer was on such a lengthy and inappropriate journey.

One thing quickly became clear to Paul. As a regular visitor to Italy he had experience of Italian driving. The Italians are not noted for their patience on the road and will make their displeasure known to any driver who holds them up by sticking to the speed limit. For the visitor, this can be alarming, as small and underpowered cars sweep past them at dangerous corners or on blind rises. But Paul noticed none of this now, and realised that the attitude of other drivers to a bulldozer was one of cautious respect. There was no point in attempting to intimidate or box-in a bulldozer. There was no point in driving too close to its rear in an attempt to get it to speed up; not only would the driver of the bulldozer not see you, but should he brake suddenly, he might not even notice the crumpling of metal as your car collided with the hardened steel outer provinces of his vehicle. In the pecking order of the Italian road, then, a bulldozer's position was evidently not to be questioned.

Of course, progress was slow, but not quite as slow as Paul had expected. As he moved upwards through the gears, Paul discovered that the bulldozer was capable of reasonable speed—perhaps that which might be achieved by a cautious Sunday motorist on a relaxed drive through the countryside. On hills this might pick up even further, as the weight of the blade helped to add momentum, even if some distance was required for a safe slow-down at the end. Only once on that journey did he feel any alarm, and that was when at the bottom of a steep hill the road bore sharply to the right without giving much warning of doing so. Paul wrestled with the steering and felt at one point that he would crash through the farmyard wall and barn directly in his path. At the last moment, though, the bulldozer negotiated the bend, the blade taking only the smallest shaving off the wall—so small, in fact, that nobody would notice, or mind if they did.

Shortly after noon he stopped in a small village. This village was slightly off the main road, and to reach it Paul was required to make a short detour. But having spotted the village from some distance away, and having seen a roadside sign advertising its single trattoria, he decided to have lunch there rather than in one of the busier towns through which his route would take him.

It was a wise choice. As he approached the village he was struck by its tranquil air. There was not much to see—a small piazza, dominated by a public building, a Baroque church, far grander than the size of such a place would normally justify, and a row of tiny shops made up the heart of the village. The trattoria was in the main piazza, its few tables sheltered in part by a couple of rickety umbrellas and in part by a couple of shaped pine trees. From the piazza several narrow alleys led into a warren of old stone houses, while behind the village groves of gnarled olive trees, bordered by the green stripes of a vineyard, stretched up to the ridge of the horizon.

Paul manoeuvred his bulldozer into the piazza, parking it in a convenient empty space beside the church. As he lowered himself out of the cab, he had the feeling that eyes were upon him, as all visitors to a village will feel, whether they arrive by bulldozer, by more conventional transport, or even by foot.

Of course, if they come by bulldozer, then they must expect curiosity to make the eyes upon them wider than normal, and this was certainly the case here. Paul's arrival reminded several inhabitants that they had been intending all along to leave the house to perform some urgent errand, and out they came, shading their eyes against the light of noon, glancing at this unconventional visitor with as much directness and frank interest as good manners allowed. In the principal shop, the *alimentari*, the owner decided that this was exactly the moment when she should give her display window a wipe and check on the state of the open boxes of tomatoes she had laid out beside her front door; from the *calzolaio*, the shoe repair shop that had long since devoted itself to the selling of newspapers, notebooks, and children's toys, the proprietor emerged on the pretext of getting a much-needed breath of fresh air. Even the village cats, tortoiseshell wraiths belonging to nobody but themselves, seemed vaguely aware that something significant was happening in the human world, and that this might even lead to that most important event in their lives—the arrival of the fishmonger's van with its candy-striped awning. These cats appeared at the same time as did the people, and it was under all these eyes, feline and human, that Paul crossed the square, pausing only briefly to admire the facade of the Baroque church.

He sat down at one of the outside tables. From within the trattoria there came the sound of a radio, but this was abruptly switched off as the owner made her appearance. She was a generously proportioned woman, somewhere in her forties, wearing a faded apron. Her hands, he noticed, bore traces of flour, which she dusted off against the apron as she approached his table.

Paul greeted her, and she returned the greeting before showing him the menu. He looked at it, quickly realising that the choice, however presented, was soup, pasta in various guises, or a single meat course.

"Of course you don't need to use the menu," said the woman. "I can make you other things. We're not very busy today." She sighed. "Or ever."

Paul smiled, and asked for a caprese salad and a bowl of pasta prepared in the manner of the region.

She nodded, and then looked over towards the bulldozer. "Working?"

Paul followed her gaze. "Just driving it," he said. It would be too complicated to explain, he thought, and nobody would believe him anyway.

The woman retreated inside, and Paul sat back in his chair, enjoying the silence. The bulldozer had been noisier than he expected, and he was pleased to have a break from the constant thudding of its diesel engine. He looked up at the sky, pale and cloudless, and saw a swallow darting against the blue, a tiny speck of air-borne energy. He closed his eyes and drew in a deep breath. He was in Italy; he was in a tiny village; he was far away from his normal world and its demands; nobody knew him here; he was free.

He heard voices, and opened his eyes. Two middle-aged men, dressed in the high-waisted trousers and rough open-necked shirts that served as the uniform of the Italian countryman, had appeared and were seating themselves at the table next to Paul's. They were followed within a very short time by two women, one of them the owner of the *alimentari* and another, much younger, from the vegetable shop on the opposite side of the piazza. Paul was aware that everybody was staring at him. They were doing this not in an unfriendly way, but with what seemed like a puzzled curiosity, politely restrained, but insistent nonetheless.

Paul inclined his head in recognition of their interest. *"Buon giorno,"* he said, not directing the greeting at anyone in particular.

This elicited a chorus of *buon giornos,* followed by a clearing of the throat by one of the middle-aged men. "Travelled far?" he asked, pointing in the direction of the bulldozer.

"Pisa," replied Paul.

There was an exchange of doubtful looks. "On that?" asked the man.

Paul nodded.

Further looks were exchanged. Then the other man spoke. "Building something?" he asked.

"No," said Paul. "Just passing through."

The *alimentari* woman leaned forward. "You're not from round here, are you?"

"No, I'm not."

"From Rome?"

Paul shook his head. "Not Rome."

"Because we've been waiting a long time to get people from Rome," she said. "They say they'll come and help us, but do they? They do not. They're too busy being bureaucrats."

"And worse," said one of the men.

"And worse," agreed the woman.

"Are you sure you're not from Rome?" asked the vegetable woman.

The other woman nudged her. "He said he wasn't. Didn't you hear him?"

"He's not from Rome," said one of the men.

"Definitely not," said the other.

They lapsed into silence. After a few minutes, the elder of

the two men said, "You see, we get hardly anybody coming here to see us. Nothing happens here—nothing, from one year's end to another."

"We harvest the grapes," said the *alimentari* woman. "We have an olive crop too, although sometimes that fails." She shrugged. "Apart from that, *niente*—nothing."

"So a visitor is always welcome," said her friend.

"Yes," said the first man. "Very welcome."

The caprese salad arrived, and Paul began to eat, watched silently by those at the neighbouring tables. It was a strange feeling—having his lunch under the eyes of this audience—but there was nothing threatening in the situation and he did not feel uneasy. He ate the pasta in similar conditions and then signalled to the owner of the trattoria that he was ready to pay the bill.

He stood up. "Well, I must continue with my journey," he said.

"One never gets anywhere unless one leaves," said the *alimentari* woman.

This was the signal for all four of his companions to get to their feet. As Paul made his way across the piazza, they walked beside him, as if they were a group of friends seeing off one of their number. When they reached the bulldozer, the *alimentari* woman reached into a bag she was carrying and took out a small cake, wrapped in muslin cloth.

"This is for you, *signore*," she said, pressing the gift into his hands. "For your journey, in case you should feel hungry."

Paul put the cake into his pocket. "You've been so kind to me," he said.

And suddenly, and quite unexpectedly, he began to weep. He felt the tears welling up and knew that he could not stop them. There was no reason for him to cry—but often our

tears have no particular justification; they are tears for something larger about the world than any private sorrow. So now
he wept for the whole notion that there should be a tiny village that nobody visited, and that there should be people
there who should be kind to a stranger. He wept for the bigger, louder world that shouted such places down; for the loss
of the small and the particular, the local and the familiar. He
wept for people who had restaurants in which few people ate
their lunch, for people who sold cheap toys and newspapers
and combs, for people who grew olive trees that failed to give
a crop, for people who thought that Rome did not really care
about them. He wept too because he had not really wept over
the loss of Becky to the personal trainer, and now at last he
could do that.

And, remarkably, they understood, and the vegetable
woman put her arms about him and embraced him and said,
"Come back and see us one day."

He wiped his tears away, burning with embarrassment
over his display. It had been a complete over-reaction to a
moment of emotion, and he felt ashamed of himself. "I'm
sorry," he said. "I was thinking of other things."

"We all cry," said the *alimentari* woman. "There is so much
to cry about."

He tried to smile. "Thank you. But I feel very stupid."

"You've lost something," said the woman.

He started to reply, but became silent, and simply nodded.
She was right; he had lost something—something that he had
thought he had possessed, but had not. And now a stranger—
somebody he had met only minutes before and whom he
would not see again—had pointed it out to him.

They stood and watched as he started the bulldozer. Then
they waved as he reversed, turned round, and began to make

his way out of the square, back towards the road that led eventually to Montalcino and the room awaiting him at the Albergo il Fiore—the Flower Inn, perched on a ridge at the edge of the village, looking down the hillside to the plains far below. He had not stayed there before, but had walked past it once and had been intrigued by the vision he had been vouchsafed, through the open front door, of two women making pasta in the kitchen beyond, rolling out the long strips of dough, stretching them between their hands like great white rubber bands. Love of what you do is unmistakable in the care with which you do it, whether it is seen in the way in which an artist applies the final touch of paint to his canvas, a master carpenter sands the last touch of roughness from the surface of the wood, or a woman making pasta kneads the compliant dough, draws it out, coaxes it to the right consistency. One day, he thought, I shall come back to this place and stay here. I shall sit in that briefly glimpsed dining room and look out through the window so high on the hill that flying birds are looked down upon from above, as angels and air travellers will see them.

5

Shaky and Impermanent Alliances

$\mathcal{H}$e narrowly avoided taking a wrong turning, just in time seeing the road sign pointing off to the right. A motorist sounded his horn and flashed his lights in protest at the suddenness of his manoeuvre, but was silenced and slipped off apologetically when Paul slowed down as if to take issue; such was the advantage of the size, weight, and brute force conferred by the bulldozer. Paul smiled; he had always been a considerate driver, patiently yielding to pushier motorists, allowing others to cut in in front of him rather than insist on his rights. Now, though, he felt tempted to assert himself and claim that priority he had never sought: a fleeting temptation, though, that did not last more than a few seconds—he could never be a convincing bully, even on a bulldozer. And so, as he made his way up the winding road to the hilltop town, he slowed down to let those behind him pass and hugged his side of the road to allow oncoming cars as much room as possible.

Through the dusty screen of his cabin, he looked up towards the cluster of buildings on the ridge of the hill. Italian hill towns are hill towns with conviction; in other places human habitation may cling to the skirts of a hill, may climb up the lower slopes while leaving the top untouched. Here the Tuscan landscape was dominated by villages and towns that had long ago chosen to occupy the most commanding available positions. The world in those days was a place of shaky and impermanent alliances; the smaller sought protection of the larger, but even the strong being subject to the vagaries of fortune, protectors might not be at hand when most needed. On a hilltop, height conferred military advantage: attackers could be seen a long way off, and could be repelled with the assistance of that most reliable of allies, gravity.

The bulldozer was slow on hills, and by the time he reached the road's last hairpin bends, he was crawling along. It was five years since he had last been there—it was just before he met Becky—but he thought he remembered there was a car park just below the town walls. As he crested the ridge he found that his memory had served him well: the car park was exactly where he had hoped it would be. There would be no point in trying to drive the bulldozer through the narrow streets around the Albergo Fiore: these were challenge enough for the tiniest of Fiats, let alone for a large piece of earth-moving equipment.

The absurdity of his situation now came home to him. On his journey he had been preoccupied with the novelty of driving the bulldozer; now the implications of what he had done dawned on him with alarming clarity. He had come to Italy in pursuit of a period of freedom, and he had lumbered himself with a ridiculously inappropriate vehicle. Had he really imagined that he could use it to visit the places he wanted to see? Had he really seen himself driving off for lunch at some neighbouring village in this yellow monster, with its throaty diesel engine and its great heavy blade? As mistakes went, it was difficult to imagine anything more ludicrous.

But it was done. Pisa was a long way away now, and he was responsible for the bulldozer until such time as he could return it to Claudio. He could take it back, of course, but that would eat into his working time, and so it made more sense to park the bulldozer and forget about it until it was time to return. He imagined that it would be safe enough: After all, who would be interested in stealing a bulldozer? Car thieves snatched cars, preferably high-powered ones, and drove them off as fast as they could, merging—they hoped— with the traffic; a bulldozer thief, if there was such a person, would have to make a very slow escape and would hardly be inconspicuous . . . It would be an easy chase for the police, thought Paul—and for a moment he saw the bulldozer with a line of police cars behind it, sirens wailing and blue lights flashing, all proceeding at bulldozer pace. The comic image cheered him, as did the thought that his situation could be far worse. He remembered the Professor's encouraging words: the important thing was that he was here, exactly where he wanted to be, in a place blessed by everything benign that Tuscany could offer. He would put the bulldozer out of his mind and concentrate on what he had come for.

The road to the parking place ran down past a bank of modern houses, an afterthought to the ancient town. There were a few cars already parked, and Paul was relieved to see that there would be space. But then he saw the sign, prominently displayed a few yards inside the entrance, with its information about parking charges and the location of the ticket machine. Temporarily abandoning the bulldozer, he walked over to the notice. Immediately he saw that he was faced with a problem. According to the list of charges, a ticket would last no more than three hours, and this meant that between the hours of eight in the morning and six in the evening, he would have to come down to the parking lot several times to feed coins into the machine. And it was far from cheap, the main point of the charges being to swell the coffers of the local commune at the expense of those wanting to park there, almost all of whom would be visitors rather than local residents.

Paul turned away from the notice in disgust. Tuscany was spacious, and there was no justification for this restrictive attitude towards parking. On his earlier visits to Italy, he had observed that people parked their cars wherever they liked—under trees, on pavements, on the side of the road; now, it seemed an altogether more orderly, somewhat more controlling attitude was making itself felt. This, he thought, must be the influence of Northern Europe, expressed through the diktats of Brussels, where the relaxed Mediterranean approach to life was frowned upon. Northern Europe liked order; Northern Europe wanted people to give receipts, to observe the law, to pay for parking—in short, to do everything that Italy had never really had the inclination to do. Italy got by on centuries-old understandings, on unwritten codes of who owed what to whom, on practices that may have been difficult to identify and explain but that worked. He sighed, and then he noticed something that he had missed when he first arrived. This was a sign, fixed to a pole rooted in a small block of concrete, saying *Paid Parking Beyond This Point.*

He stared at the notice for a minute or two. If paid parking started beyond it, then, by perfectly reasonable inference, parking on this side was free. There was not much room before the point at which paid parking began—indeed, although there was room for motorcycles, there was not enough for a car . . . unless, of course, the paid parking notice were to be pushed a bit further into the car park. That would create space for a couple of cars—or one bulldozer—to park free of charge in the now-expanded unregulated zone.

His eyes moved down to the concrete block. It was not small, and would certainly be far too heavy for anybody to lift. Even two or three men, he imagined, would find it hard to shift; but if one were to have a bulldozer . . .

He climbed back into the cab. Looking about him, he saw that he appeared to be on his own. A man who had just parked at the other end of the car park was now walking off towards the town centre; a small van, laden with vegetables, laboured up the approach road, going in the opposite direction; somewhere in the distance, perhaps in one of the olive groves, a buzz saw whined. There was nobody about.

He reached forward to switch on the ignition. *Always have the engine running when you operate the blade* . . . He remembered the gist of Claudio's advice. He had said something about hydraulics too, but that was just by way of explanation. The main thing was to have the engine running, which he now had.

He put his hand on the lever that operated the blade. *Towards me, up* . . . But the blade was already up, and had been in that position all along. *Forward, then* . . . He eased the lever. At first it did nothing, but when he increased the pressure, it started to move. There was the sound of whirring somewhere—perhaps from the hydraulic pump, he decided. This sound increased, and then, very slowly, the blade began to descend towards the ground. He took his hand off the lever and it stopped. Gently he pushed again and it moved once more.

Now the blade was only a few inches off the ground. Paul lifted his hand from the lever altogether and put the bulldozer into gear. Moving with the blade lowered gave a slightly different sensation to the driver, making him feel as if the bulldozer was leaning forward; but it was responsive enough and was easily manoeuvred into position immediately in front of the concrete block and its sign.

Paul took a deep breath. What he was about to do was illegal, and he could not recall ever deliberately breaking the law before, or at least breaking it in this calculated way. And breaking one's own laws was one thing; breaking the laws of a foreign country was quite another. He wondered what offence he was committing. He was aware of Italy's Criminal Code—he knew about it from his days in Florence; he had shared a room with a law student who always seemed to have his nose buried in the *Codice Penale*. What did the code say about unlawfully moving concrete blocks that were the property of the Comune di Montalcino—and doing so with the intention of avoiding a legitimate charge?

He knew from reading the newspapers that those who disappeared into the maw of the Italian criminal justice system could be trapped there for years, even when their offence was a petty one. There were endless procedural complications, often of Byzantine complexity, and understood only by lawyers—and not by all lawyers at that. There were appeals that dragged on and on, working their way up through layer after layer of courts—and frequently lasting for decades. And at the end of the day, unless you were a politician and for this reason exempt from punishment, there were Italian jails where you would be surrounded by people like Occhidilupo, who would be related by an elaborate system of cousinage to everybody else in the prison, but not to you. Of course very few people were actually incarcerated: the Italian justice system allowed sentences to be served at home, and if home were a villa on the Amalfi coast, or a bucolic farmhouse in an olive grove, then that would have to do, and for many it did. And then there was the moral question. Was it *right* to move a public sign, even a very short distance? Parking regulations might seem petty, but they were part of the system of rules that made human society possible—a clause in the social contract without which, as Hobbes had warned, life would be nasty, brutish, and short. Paul thought of Hobbes, and imagined him watching him reproachfully, ready to witness yet another infringement. He sighed. He had not asked for this bulldozer—he had taken it solely to avoid giving offence to the Professor and Claudio, both of whom were patently decent people only trying to help. So if one were to weigh his actions in some notional scales of justice, surely a minor twisting—or, in this case perhaps, pushing—of a rule would be offset by the greater good of not hurting the feelings of others.

And then the solution occurred to him. The answer, when it presented itself, struck him as morally unassailable: he would not try to evade payment of the parking charge—rather he would calculate what it would cost each day were he to pay it at the ticket machine. Then, having worked that out, he would multiply that figure by the appropriate number of days (allowing for Sundays, during which parking was free) and give that exact sum of money to the Comune, leaving it in an envelope under their door before he left. In that way he would not be depriving the town of its due.

He smiled to himself. That was it: nobody, not even Thomas Hobbes, could fault him; nobody could accuse him of anything criminal. The moving of the sign would be no more than a temporary expedient that would, in the result, lead to the civic authorities collecting more money than they otherwise would. This was because if he did not move the sign and went off to park his bulldozer beyond the town boundaries, that income would be lost to the public purse. So doing what he was proposing to do was not only convenient to him, but an act of generosity to the town itself. There was a useful word for that—one that he remembered from his schooldays, when he would sometimes page through the dictionary to find words to display in essays, like trophies: it would be a *supererogatory* act. He had loved that word, and now he could use it again after those long-ago sixteen-year-old ramblings. Supererogatory: more than was required by duty . . . it was a perfect fit.

His conscience now clear, Paul inched the bulldozer forward. There was a slight jolt as the blade encountered the concrete, but then slowly, and with an odd rasping sound, the block began to move. The pole swayed a bit, and Paul was momentarily concerned that it might fall over, but it soon steadied itself. Then he stopped. He had shifted the notice about three yards and this created just enough room for him to reverse the bulldozer into the space opened up. It was the perfect place—shaded by a tree and in no way impeding the entry of other cars into the parking lot.

He raised the blade before switching off the engine. Once again there was a satisfying whirring sound from the hydraulic system as the blade lifted. Everything worked, and Paul felt a sudden affection for this curious vehicle that had brought him to his destination. He decided there was a lot to be said for bulldozers. They were *honest* vehicles—honest in the sense that they did not purport to be anything other than what they were. They were not about luxury or speed; they did what they were meant to do and no more. They made no statement; they said nothing about the people who drove them. They earned their living and made no demands.

The car park was still deserted as Paul followed the path to the town above. He was travelling fairly light even if he was planning to spend some weeks away from home, and had fitted all his clothes and personal effects into one soft-sided suitcase and all the papers and files for his book into another. Now, balanced with a suitcase in each hand, he began to make his way up to the road circling the town walls and that led to his hotel. He paused halfway, putting the suitcases down for a few minutes while he recovered his breath and looked down the hillside. He saw olive trees. He saw more hills, blue and distant, and a line of cypresses on the horizon. He looked up at the sky, empty and filled with a lambent blue. He wanted to break into song, but did not, of course, although nobody minds—or is surprised—if you break into song in Italy; and so he continued his short journey, ten minutes later finding himself standing at the door of the Fiore. Somewhere inside, in the cool darkness of the hotel, a woman was singing. He listened: her voice had the purity that comes with being an amateur who has had a smattering of training; he did not want her to stop.

There was a sign that read *Reception,* and beneath it a desk. He put down his suitcases and looked about him. On the wall behind the desk was a framed picture, brightly coloured, of the Montalcino coat of arms. It was an indication of the civic pride that sustains every small Italian town—except those few that have given up because everyone has gone away. *Campanilismo*—the devotion to the local, often exaggerated, was the patriotism that counted in Italy, outdoing the claims of any wider national feeling. My *campanile,* my bell tower, is bigger and more glorious than yours . . .

"*Buon giorno . . .*"

A woman had appeared almost unnoticed, and was greeting him with a smile. The singing had stopped.

"I was enjoying your song," he said. "*Maremma amara?*"

She clapped her hands in delight. "You knew it! And you speak Italian!"

"Poorly."

"Nonsense. You could be taken for one of us."

He made a gesture of acceptance. "You're very kind. But it's a rather sad song, that one, isn't it?"

"I wasn't feeling sad, I was just remembering how we learned it at school. Everybody does—at least around here. And Maremma is no longer the hard place it used to be—so that makes it a little less sad."

They moved on to his reservation. "You're going to be with us for a good long time," she said, looking at the register. "When they made the booking for you, I wondered why you would want to spend so long here."

It was a polite way of enquiring, and he told her. "I'm working on something." He made a scribbling movement. "Writing."

She nodded. "We often have writers here. I think they enjoy the peacefulness."

"Yes, of course."

"And our wine . . ."

He laughed. "Perhaps the two go together."

She filled in a form and handed it to him. "We've put you in the best room. It's one that looks down over the valley."

"You're very kind," he said.

She showed him to his room. As they climbed the stairs, she asked him whether he had a car. "Since you're staying for so long, we might be able to arrange somewhere for you to park."

"I have something," he said. "But I've found somewhere for it." It was too complicated to explain; he could hardly say, "I have a bulldozer."

They entered the room. The window was open, the air clean and cool, freshened by the several hundred metres that lay between the town and the floor of the valley below.

"We have given you a table," she said, pointing to a simple desk that had been placed against a wall. "As the woman who made the reservation asked." She hesitated. "Your wife, perhaps?"

Paul shook his head. "My editor."

"Your wife has stayed in Scotland? She doesn't like Italy?"

"No wife," said Paul. "I'm single."

She looked apologetic.

"Sort of," Paul continued. "I was with somebody, but then . . ."

She touched his arm lightly. "I'm sure there'll be someone else. All in good time."

He thanked her for providing the table. "This will be a wonderful place to work," he said. "This view . . . I'll have to be careful that I don't sit here all day and look out over the valley." He paused. "You didn't give me your name."

"I'm Elena Sabatino," she said. "Everybody calls me Ella, which was the name of my grandmother too. My daughter's also called Ella. The women in our family have been Ella all the way back. Right back to the time when the Florentines . . ."

At the mention of the Florentines, he lowered his eyes. "A terrible time," he said.

She gave him a searching glance. "So you understand?"

He nodded. "I've read the history books." He had, but was a bit hazy on the details—and the dates. The Florentines had laid siege to Montalcino in . . . when was it? The sixteenth century? Yesterday, in Italian terms.

She shook her head. "It was a long time ago, and people should forget. But they don't, you know."

"So much has happened in history."

It was an anodyne remark, but it served its purpose, and the Florentines were temporarily forgotten. Ella moved on to a discussion of the times when meals would be served and the arrangements for the opening of the front door should he come in late at night.

"I doubt if I'll be in late," he said.

She shrugged. "You never know. This is a place where the unexpected happens."

"Of course."

She continued, "Which is what makes life interesting, would you not say, *dottore*?"

"Please, not *dottore*, Paul. Or, if you wish, Paolo." He understood Italian formality, but he found the constant use of *dottore* tiresome. It was a title given to any graduate, or to anybody whom people suspected might be a graduate. In fact, as a friend had explained to him when he first went to live in Florence, *dottore* sometimes seemed to be a courtesy title for anybody who wore glasses . . . "And it's better to err on the side of caution," the same friend had said. "Always address a *tenente* as *Capitano;* always address a *conte* as *Principe*. If demotion always hurts, promotion invariably pleases."

She handed him the key. "You'll be very happy here, Paolo. People usually are."

6

A Simple Dish of Beans and Strong, Home-Cured Sausage

*H*e awoke the next day to the tolling of a bell. The sound came in waves, growing slightly louder and then receding, as if the person puling at the bell rope was tiring, summoning up energy, and then returning to the task with renewed vigour. Paul unlatched the wooden shutters and let the daylight flood into his room. Opening the window itself, he filled his lungs with air that bore the scents of the morning, of trees and vines, of the stone of the houses warmed by the sun, of wood smoke from a fire somewhere. It was the scent of place, the subtle signature of an entire landscape. It was the smell of Tuscany.

The bell made its final announcement—a last, half-hearted strike that was followed by silence. This was broken by a sudden burst of song from a bird concealed in the foliage below the window. He looked down: directly beneath him, two floors lower, was the hotel garden. This was an irregularly shaped piece of land that dropped sharply down to the next building, of which only the red-tiled roof was visible. Thereafter the village continued its descent of the hill until it reached the strip of olive trees marking the start of the vineyards.

He saw the church off to the side, its bell tower projecting above a cluster of rooftops. He remembered being told on his last visit that it was disused, and had been acquired by one of the town's quarters as a venue for communal dinners and meetings. That was not an undignified fate for a church, he thought, and the bell, at least, had survived—a reminder of a time when the divisions of the day were marked by peals. And to such a sound he had now awoken—it was infinitely better, he felt, than the electronic buzz of an alarm clock.

Ella had told him that breakfast would be served in the small dining room at the foot of the stairs, but that if he preferred to go elsewhere, the café in the main piazza would have fresh pastries from the town bakery. He had decided on that, and after a quick shower in the tiny bathroom attached to his room, he made his way out into the street. On a corner directly opposite the hotel a statue of the Madonna, set back into a wall, looked down on passers-by with that other-worldly, slightly dreamy gaze that Marian figures affect so effortlessly. At the foot of this figure, just low enough for somebody to reach on tiptoes, was a small shelf for offerings of flowers. A tiny wilted posy, the sort of thing a child might pick, lay on this shelf along with a square of delicate printed tissue paper in which *amarettini* are wrapped: an offering, too, perhaps, that the Madonna had discreetly consumed overnight.

He remembered the Caffé Fiaschetteria Italiana from his last visit. The Art Deco ornamentation of the café, with its red velvet benches and ornate mirrors, was not what one expected in a Tuscan hilltop town, but had made it the pride of Montalcino's citizens; Florence, Venice might have their treasures, but so do we, and as long as you have one fine place to sit and review the world, then that will suffice. You cannot be in more than one place at a time, can you?

He found a table indoors, as those directly outside the café were occupied by early arrivals. Two groups of visitors, German and Swedish, were already ensconced under the umbrellas, and were watching the public strolling with which Italy begins the day, the precursor of the evening ritual of the *passeggiata.* Those inside seemed more local: a couple of men who had interrupted their work in the vineyards to come into town for equipment and a chance to speak to friends; a woman in business dress, a briefcase of papers by her side; a late-teenage boy and his girlfriend engaged in urgent, whispered conversation. Paul looked at the teenagers; the boy looked worried, as the girl's gestures made clear her displeasure. He wondered about the boy's offence: insensitivity, perhaps; looking at other girls; not returning a phone call. There were so many ways a relationship could go wrong, and the young man was probably only now discovering them.

He ordered a cup of milky coffee and an almond croissant. The pleasure he had felt on waking up that morning—the sheer delight of being in a place like this, free of the restraints of home—had not faded. If anything, it was stronger. The day stretched ahead of him—a day in which he could please himself as to what he did. He knew that he had to work—he had told himself that he must put in at least three hours a day at his desk—but for the rest he was at liberty to walk, to read, or simply to sit in a café if he so wished. Italy was full of people who simply sat in cafés, he reminded himself, and few of them seemed to be unhappy or anxious—apart from young men, perhaps, whose girlfriends were now shaking a finger in admonition.

His coffee and croissant arrived, and at the same time a man came in and sat down at the table next to his. Paul glanced at him and nodded a greeting. The Fiaschetteria Italiana might have sophisticated ambitions, but this was still a small town, and people greeted one another in the way of small towns everywhere.

His neighbour was a man in his late forties, dressed smartly but not in a way that suggested he was bound for work. He had a copy of the newspaper *La Nazione*, which he laid down on the table with a sigh.

"A fine day," said the man. He spoke cautiously, articulating the words with care.

Paul looked out through the doorway. "Not a cloud," he said.

The response caused relief. "You speak Italian . . . But may I ask where are you from?"

Paul told him.

"I shall never get to Scotland," said the man, rather wistfully. "I am a great devotee of *Lucia di Lammermoor*, but I shall never get to Scotland."

Paul smiled. "You never know."

This brought a shaking of the head. "No, I can't get away from Italy—from here. I have aged relatives, you see—they live here in Montalcino, in Siena itself, down in Grosseto—all over the place, in fact. I am the one they telephone every day, never my brother." He paused. "I should introduce myself. I am Fellini—Onesto Fellini. That is my burden, I'm afraid."

Paul was tactful. "I see nothing . . ."

"Oh no, I'm afraid it is not the easiest of names. Onesto is usually a surname in Italy, but these things migrate. And Fellini is common enough, but I still think of Federico Fellini and his films. If some famous person has your name, you're always in his shadow. Always."

Paul shrugged. "I didn't think of him when you gave me your name."

"The difficulty," continued Onesto, "is that I'm the local

schoolteacher—or one of them. I'm the principal of the school, you see, and children find a name like Onesto very amusing."

Paul took a sip of his coffee.

"I mustn't disturb you," said Onesto. "Not everybody comes in here to talk."

Paul assured him that he did not mind. "I enjoy conversation. It enables me to use my Italian—a language gets rusty, you know." He paused. "I suppose everything we know goes that way."

Onesto nodded his agreement. "It certainly does. One of the subjects I teach is mathematics. The children go off on their school holidays—they're on holiday now, of course—and they come back and they seem to have forgotten all I taught them." He smiled. "My predecessor retired rather late. He went on and on, teaching several generations. Towards the end he found himself forgetting what he had taught the children the previous term, and they forgot it too—so nobody remembered anything."

Onesto picked up *La Nazione*. "The world," he said, with a sigh, gesturing to a headline. "Politicians and their tricks. Wars. Floods. Bad accidents. That's our world, isn't it?"

"It's the world that people report."

Onesto shook his head. "They report it because that's what people want to read. Nobody wants to read good news. *Thousands of planes land safely* is very dull news. *Plane misses runway altogether* is much better."

He opened a page. "You see here?" Onesto pointed to a news item at the top of the page. "This is a row about the disappearance of municipal funds in Florence. Where have the millions gone? they ask. I can tell you. Everybody can tell you. They've gone into the pockets of that scoundrel in the photograph. He's the one who's asking the question, but he's the one who knows the answer best of all." He made an explosive and dismissive sound. "Pah! Italy!"

"It's not just you," said Paul; he was used to the self-deprecation of the Italians.

"Perhaps not," began Onesto. "Of course there are others . . ."

Paul did not hear the rest. He had seen another headline. It was below the report on the Florentine funds, and set in smaller type. *Occhidilupo Escapes.*

Onesto noticed his frown. "Something wrong?"

Paul asked him for the newspaper. "Something there . . ." He took it from Onesto and began to read aloud.

"Police authorities in Pisa revealed that Calogero Occhidilupo (38), currently under judicial investigation for multiple crimes, had escaped from his cell at Carabinieri Headquarters in the city. Occhidilupo overpowered his guard and fled through an unsecured window at the rear of the Carabinieri barracks. Extensive searches have been undertaken, including a raid on Occhidilupo's last-known house in the Province of Siena, but these have so far proved fruitless."

Paul stopped reading, and looked at Onesto. "I met that man," he said. "It's a complicated story, but I was briefly detained—briefly *and* wrongfully—in Pisa after I arrived. I shared a cell with him—just for a few hours, but it was definitely him."

Onesto took the newspaper from him. Glancing at the photograph beneath the report, he let out a whistle. "Him!" he exclaimed.

"He looks the part, doesn't he?" said Paul.

"Oh yes," said Onesto. "He's the real thing, all right. Every bit the traditional brigand." He paused, and then tapped at the photograph. "He'll be returning to his old haunts, I expect. He's carried out every sort of crime you could name—and some you couldn't." He nodded in the direction of the road below. "Pisa was a bit off his usual beat, I think. They picked him up because there had been a spate of robberies over there." He paused. "He has a woman down near San Antimo. That's the place they'll have searched."

Paul listened with growing fascination. How could they have allowed Occhidilupo to escape from the very heart of the Carabinieri barracks? And how could somebody as immediately recognisable as this bandit expect to avoid recapture in a society as watchful of others as rural Italy? "So where do you think he'll be?"

The teacher thought for a moment. "In the woods," he said. "He'll have found somewhere to hide. If wild boars can do it—and there are plenty of them—then a wily creature like Occhidilupo will have no trouble doing the same."

Onesto made a gesture towards the door—towards the piazza and beyond. It was a gesture that seemed to say *Here we're safe; out there, though . . .* But then something seemed to occur to him. "They could get the dogs after him," he mused. "Plenty of dogs round here."

Paul had seen dogs—small, pampered dogs of fussy breed—being walked in the street by their owners, but he could imagine Occhidilupo making short work of them. "I've seen them . . ."

Onesto cut him short. "Oh, not those dogs," he said dismissively. "Not them." He went on to explain that people kept dogs—much larger dogs—to take part in boar hunts. Boars damaged the vineyards, he said, and every so often there would be an organised hunt, with scores of local men taking part.

"It's a very noisy occasion," Onesto continued. "You hear the howling for miles around. The dogs love it, of course—it's what they live for. Dogs are very easily caught up in human enthusiasms. And they're so trusting—aren't they? We can lead them astray very easily."

They both fell silent. Then Paul asked, "Will he . . . strike again?" He knew he sounded melodramatic, but the whole story of Occhidilupo had a surrealistic, unlikely tone to it. Did brigands still exist? It seemed that they did—at least in Italy. And every country had its outlaws: India had its *dacoits,* the Malacca Straits its pirates, and America its Mob. Occhidilupo, perhaps, was a universal human type.

Onesto answered in a matter-of-fact way. "Yes, undoubtedly. Somebody will stumble across him and he'll . . ." He made a throat-slitting gesture.

Paul drew in his breath. "Really?"

"But naturally."

The silence returned.

Onesto folded his newspaper. "So be careful," he said.

*P*aul returned to the hotel, unsettled by his conversation with Onesto. Of course he had enjoyed the opportunity to talk to a local—particularly to somebody who would be as well-informed as a schoolteacher—but the discussion of Occhidilupo had introduced an ominous note. And then there had been the mention of hunting dogs . . . Paul imagined what it was like to hear their braying as they led their owners through the woods; surely one of the most frightening sounds to the human ear, the sound of animals in pursuit of their prey—especially when the prey happened to be oneself.

He had already arranged his day, conscious that this was

not a holiday, but a working trip. He had assured Gloria that the manuscript would be ready for the copy-editor by the time he returned, and he intended to keep that promise. Three hours at his desk were to be followed by a visit to a vineyard. This had been set up through a telephone conversation the previous evening with a contact in the *Consorzio*, the body that ran the affairs of the wine producers and organised visits for any wine writers on a pilgrimage to the area: Paul had allocated twelve pages of the new book to the wines of the region and had already filled six with an account of the growth of their reputation in the last decades of the twentieth century. This was to precede a more personal section—an account of the experience of a typical wine producer of the region, Antonio Bartolo del Bosco. When the *Consorzio* official had suggested the estate, Paul had demurred. "I'm sure he runs a very good place," he said as tactfully as he could, "but might it not be better to visit one of the better-known producers?" He was suddenly aware of his tactlessness. "No offence intended to Signor Barto . . ."

"Bartolo del Bosco."

This was followed by a brief silence at the other end of the telephone, and by a revelation.

"He's my cousin."

"Of course, of course. Well, I very much look forward to meeting him. And . . . and I'm sure he's very typical."

"Yes, he is." The official continued: "You'll like him, you know. Everybody does—and his wine's much better than some . . . than some unkind people say." There was a further pause. "He's from a family of great distinction and immense antiquity, you know. You'll see."

The hours at the desk passed quickly. There was more work for him to do than he had imagined: reading through his manuscript in review, he realised that large sections of it had a heaviness about it, a dullness, that had not been present in his previous books. He suspected that this was probably a result of his state of mind at the time. The book had been started before Becky left, but he had not been far into it when the relationship began to unravel. If there was no sparkle in the manuscript, and that, the press had noted, was the hallmark of his books—a certain infectious delight in the discovery of new places and the food and wine that went with them—then that absence must be down to the absence of precisely that curiosity and engagement in his private life. But how did one add sparkle to a life from which that very quality had drained away? By coming here, he thought; by coming here to Montalcino and allowing the beauty of the Tuscan countryside to work its magic; by doing exactly what he was now doing.

He turned his head slightly to look out of the window. He knew that windows could be the enemy of writers, being places out of which to gaze while you should instead be working. But not this window; this seemed to have the opposite effect, as the view it afforded of the hillside below, and beyond that of distant hills and sky, lifted his spirits, allowing him to approach his manuscript with renewed enthusiasm. He would somehow capture the feel of his surroundings— the quiet satisfaction of life on the land, the rhythms, the sense of history—of things having been for centuries the way they were now. All of that was tangible enough when you walked about the streets of Montalcino, and if he could somehow convey that when he wrote about Tuscan cuisine, then he would have achieved what he wanted. And he would do it.

He looked at the page of typescript before him, and drew

a line through it. Then, in the margin, he wrote: *Start again,* taking delight in the heroic firmness of the words. These were not the words of somebody who was procrastinating— they were the words of one who was going to finish what he had come to finish, and finish it well. With his laptop computer waiting obediently, he began to type: "The point about wild mushrooms is that they will grow where *they* want to grow, not where *you* want them to grow. In the woods that climb up the hill of a small Tuscan village, you may meet people over the weekend, sometimes whole families, foraging for the mushrooms they suspect are hiding under a covering of leaves, behind a slight ridge in the ground . . ." *Yes!* It was exactly the right beginning. He closed his eyes and for a moment imagined the Italian mushroom hunters combing the woods around Montalcino; he saw a man crouching over a find, the fungus in his hands, dusting at it with the small brush that comes at the end of an Italian mushroom-hunting penknife, before popping his trophy into a shoulder bag. This was the texture of the life that he would describe in *Paul Stuart's Tuscan Table*—a life led in close proximity to the gifts of nature, to the produce that would end up on that very table. He wrote a note to himself: *Mushroom, mushroom knife with brush . . .*

He worked for slightly longer than the three hours he had planned. When he heard the tolling of the bell from the church below, he was surprised by how quickly time had passed. Yet he had written more than he had hoped and rose from his desk with a sense of achievement. He had pinned a map of the surrounding area to the wall, and now he consulted this to find the precise location of the Castello Riccio estate. They had given him general instructions over the telephone as to how to find it; it was, they said, not far away at all, a short distance down the road to Sant'Angelo in Colle. Now, however, the map told a different story, and Paul realised that what he imagined would be a walk of half an hour or so, manageable even in the midday heat, was likely to take a good few hours on foot.

He thought about the bulldozer. His earlier idea of using it as his main means of getting about had faded, and he had been wondering about taxis. There was a village taxi service—he had seen the car in question parked outside a vegetable shop—but if he resorted to that as a means of getting out to Castello Riccio, then he would either have to walk all the way back or, at the end of his visit, summon the taxi. The problem was that the taxi could turn out to be unreliable, or hard to contact, or disinclined to make the journey. Not all taxi drivers, Paul had discovered, actually *wanted* to take passengers to their destination; some of them, he felt, were in it for the arguments, or the opportunity to pontificate, or for the sheer pleasure of driving past those trying to summon them at the road edge.

He made up his mind. What was the point of having a bulldozer if you were not going to make at least some use of it? He needed to get around in order to finish his book, and that meant he would have to use what transport he had; people could stare if they wished; he would use the bulldozer *with conviction*.

He saw Ella on his way out.

"So, you're off on your researches?" she remarked.

"Yes. Castello Riccio. A wine place. You know it?"

His question was answered with a strange noise. It might have been speech—perhaps a rare word in the local dialect, an obscure shibboleth Paul would never know; or it could have been a simple clearing of the throat.

He waited for something more to be said, but Ella remained silent.

"Well," said Paul at last, "that's what I'm doing."

This prompted Ella to say something further. "Poor Tonio. So sad."

Paul raised an eyebrow. At least Tonio was less of a mouthful than Antonio Bartolo del Bosco. "Why? Why do you say 'sad'?"

She began to explain, but broke off, and finished with a shrug. "He tries," she said.

Paul waited for her to expand on this, but she looked at her watch, and smiled. "Books need to be written—and the hotel needs to be cleaned." She paused. "Will we see you for dinner?"

Paul nodded. "I hope so."

"*Fagioli con salsiccia?*" she asked.

"Perfect," said Paul. Beans with sausage would be just right at the end of a working day—and he would bring it into his chapter the following morning. "*Cucina povera,*" he would write. "The poor kitchen. At the heart of this Tuscan tradition of plain cooking lie beans in all their simplicity. And what better than a simple dish of beans and strong, home-cured sausage, washed down with a glass of Chianti while the sun sets on the distant hills and the last of the homing birds dart across the sky . . ."

She thought of something. "If I give you something for Tonio—a cake, a simple *castagnaccio*—would you mind taking it to him? You'll be driving there, I take it?"

Paul hesitated. "Yes." He did not need to explain. And it was true; he would be driving. "Yes, I'd be delighted."

"Poor man," she muttered as she went off into the kitchen to collect the cake. "Tonio, I mean. Not you. Tonio. Poor man."

7

You Can Never Eat Enough Garlic

$\mathcal{H}$e made his way to the car park. From the road circling the town walls he looked down on the neat line of parked cars; there at the end, in its specially created space, was the bulldozer. He paused and took in the sight, unable to stop himself grinning. Whatever disadvantages there were to driving around Italy on a bulldozer, there was the undoubted pleasure of having a story to tell in the future. *You may not believe this, but I travelled around Tuscany on a bulldozer . . .* People would be incredulous, but he would make sure he had a photograph to prove it. He would get somebody to take a picture of him at the controls, perhaps with the blade lowered, to show that he had actually used it for what it was intended. He might even use it in his book—*the author in Tuscany, on his bulldozer . . .* Author photographs were predictable, and often dull, showing the writer at his desk or, in the case of cookery books, at the chopping board; this would be refreshingly different.

As he approached the entrance to the car park, he saw something that caused him concern. A uniformed attendant, a young woman sporting a white-topped cap at a jaunty angle, was walking along the lines of parked cars, peering at the tickets that the drivers had put out for display. She was paying special attention to one car in particular, and now she extracted a pad from her bag and began to write. Paul hesitated. If he went in now, she would see him getting onto the bulldozer and might well question him about it. Perhaps she had already issued him with a ticket, or had even called the police to report the moving of the sign. He stood for some time in indecision, as he thought of another possibility. If he were to start the bulldozer within the next few minutes, the attendant would still be engaged in finding her victim and might not bother with him. He made up his mind and walked quickly and purposefully through the car park gate.

He did not look at the attendant, but busied himself with climbing up into the bulldozer cabin and starting the engine. It fired immediately. Then he glanced over towards the attendant and saw she was looking in his direction. As their eyes met, she raised her hand in a cheerful wave. He waved back and engaged first gear.

He had studied a map before leaving the hotel and had located Castello Riccio. The estate lay just off the road that followed the ridge of hills, dropping slightly as it neared Sant'Angelo in Colle. This small village, perched on its own hill, was at the south-west end of the Brunello zone of production, and was far quieter and less popular with visitors than Montalcino itself. Now, in the shimmering heat of the early afternoon, it was blue, as distant hills might appear in a watercolour. When it first came into view, Paul stopped for a while, steering the bulldozer to the verge of the road. Switching off the engine, he sat in the cab, enjoying the sights and sounds of the countryside. The vegetation at the roadside was scrub bush—wild brambles, small shrubs, and a sort of creeping vine with vivid heart-shaped leaves—but beyond that, only a few yards away, was an olive grove sloping down to a small farmhouse in the distance.

The air was filled with the insistent protests of insects. This sound rose and fell in waves; at its highest point it was almost deafening, like a persistent and incorrigible natural tinnitus, but it would ebb into a background hum before rising once more in protest. A couple of cars passed, but otherwise Paul was on his own.

After sitting there for ten minutes, Paul resumed his journey. Castello Riccio was only a short way beyond the turn-off to Sant'Angelo in Colle and was marked by a large sign on which an elaborate family crest had been painted. The main feature of this crest was a picture of a castle in a state of disrepair; on one side of this castle was a wild boar, tusks and all, while on the other was a wood. Beneath all these, forming the base of the crest, was a picture of an ancient leather-bound book, open to show illuminated pages.

His destination could be seen from the turn-off—a large farmhouse with a few outbuildings scattered about it. One of the largest of these had a new roof, the tiles a lighter red than those on the other buildings; this, Paul assumed, was the *cantina* where the wine was made and stored. A truck parked beside it, laden with crates, confirmed this. Behind the buildings was a small stand of oak trees, and beyond these, climbing up the slope of a gradual hill, were the vines themselves. As always in the Tuscan countryside, there was no sign of activity when the scene was viewed from afar; a stillness, suited to the heat and the unmoving air, reigned over the buildings, the yard, the vines, and Paul knew that it was only when one came close up that activity would be made out.

He parked the bulldozer under a tree a short distance from the house. There was still no sign of anybody, but when he approached the front door, his footsteps crunching on the gravel of the path, a posse of dogs, small and indignant, rushed out to bark. The dogs kept their distance, but they had served to alert their owner, who now appeared first at a ground-floor window, and then in the front doorway. *Tonio,* thought Paul. That grand, cumbersome name, and then just this man . . .

Paul greeted Tonio and began to introduce himself.

"I know who you are," Tonio said. "I had a telephone call. They told me you were coming."

Paul saw that Tonio was a man somewhere in his fifties, perhaps slightly older, with a shock of brown hair and thick eyebrows. His eyes were bright, and Paul immediately warmed to his smile. There was about him, though, a rather resigned look, with a suggestion of being weighed down by the ages. Paul remembered the crest with its ancient castle and its old book; family history could sit heavily on the shoulders of one destined to keep a name, and a place, alive.

Tonio led Paul through the hallway into a large room that seemed to act as living room and office. Against a wall at the far end was a desk on which piles of paper had been neatly stacked; before the desk was a chair of aged dark oak with carved legs; a jacket hung over the back of this chair, giving it the air of having been recently vacated. Two of the walls were lined with book-shelves and the other two were covered with pictures darkened with age—a holy family on the flight into Egypt, a boy with a hunting dog, a woman filling a pitcher from a spring.

Paul's host invited him to sit down on a defeated-looking sofa while he drew up a library chair. "I'm relieved that you speak Italian," he began. "Most of the visitors sent out to us do not, and we have to rely on my less-than-perfect English. I make many mistakes, I fear, sometimes to the great confusion of our visitors. Italian and English have false friends in their vocabulary."

"Oh, I've done the same thing," said Paul.

"I can't imagine that."

Paul looked up at the vaulted ceiling. This was painted, but the pigment had faded and only vague shapes and outlines remained. Tonio noticed his gaze and offered an explanation. "Scenes from the Risorgimento," he said. "Camillo di Cavour in Piedmont, plotting against the Austrians. Unfortunately, we had a flood in the room above this one some years ago, and the water lifted off much of the plaster, including all of the Austrians. We had to restore it as best we could."

"So your family has been here a long time?" said Paul.

He noticed the question had an effect on his host. It was as if he had been asked a troubling question and had been forced to trawl through memory for the answer. Eventually Tonio replied. "A long time, yes; some centuries, in fact. Before that we were in le Marche—hence the name."

Paul frowned. "Forgive me, the reference . . ."

Tonio smiled. "Bartolo, you will recall, was a great jurist from those parts. He lived in the *trecento*—what you call the fourteenth century. I believe we may be descended from his family, although there is still much research to be done."

May be descended . . . it was all rather vague. Or *shall soon be descended;* Paul remembered di Lampedusa's parvenu who, if he did not already have distinguished ancestors, was said to be in the process of getting them . . .

Paul mentioned the crest and the open book. This seemed to please Tonio. "So many people don't look at these things. They forget that the whole history of a family might be displayed right there—in one or two simple devices on a *stemma*. You saw the book, which is the *Digest* of Justinian."

"I see."

Tonio continued his explanation. "Justinian was the Eastern Roman Emperor—over in Constantinople. He built Hagia Sophia—you may have been there—that great church that the Turks stole from us and made into a mosque. And he collected the writings of Roman jurists."

He paused, as if to allow Paul time to catch up with the vast sweep of history. "I believe there may be some family connection with Justinian," he said. "These things are obscure, of course, and I would not lay too much emphasis on it—but I believe it may exist."

Paul expressed admiration. "It must be a great responsibility," he said. "Looking after a place with that amount of history behind it."

Tonio accepted the compliment gravely, bowing his head in acknowledgement. Pointing to a line of framed photographs on one of the lower shelves, he explained that they were pictures of more recent generations, of uncles and aunts, of his grandfather. His grandfather, he said, was a particularly talented winemaker but had been denied the success he deserved. "They were envious, of course. Envy is a very big factor in Italy, you know. Everyone is envious of everyone else. It has always been so."

Paul sympathised. "In Scotland too. We call it the tall poppy syndrome. If somebody does anything exceptional, then others will want to cut him down to size. Chopping the head off the tall poppy, you see."

Tonio laughed. "That is a very good metaphor. I will remember that." He made to rise to his feet. "Would you like to see the *cantina*?"

They left the house and went into the building that Paul had seen when he turned off the road. As they were making their way there, Tonio suddenly stopped. He had not spotted the bulldozer under the tree and now noticed it for the first time.

"You came on that, Signor Stuart?"

Paul smiled. "I know it's very unusual, but I've been using it to get around. I rented it."

Tonio looked at him in frank astonishment. "You've been driving a bulldozer?"

"It's not as slow as you'd imagine."

Tonio whistled. "Astonishing! I've heard that Englishmen are eccentric, but this . . ."

"Scotsman."

"Forgive me, Scotsmen too. I cannot imagine that any-body else would use a bulldozer in that way. Amazing!"

They continued on their way to the *cantina*. In the cool of the building Paul saw the tanks and the casks of wine stacked neatly on large racks, each with its date noted in chalk.

"Last year was an especially good vintage," said Tonio. "We shall sample it and you shall see what I mean."

He moved towards a large cask lying on a rough wooden trestle. He picked up a pipette and examined it against the light from a window. Then he turned to Paul.

"Forgive me for asking, Signor Stuart, but are you . . ." He tapped the pipette gently against the palm of his hand. "Are you familiar with Italian wine?"

Paul was surprised. He assumed that the *Consorzio* official had told him that he wrote on the subject. "I do my best," he said. "It's a complex subject."

Tonio smiled. "Yes, very complex indeed. It's just that there are many people who think that Italian wine is Chianti, and Soave maybe. That flabby stuff. They think that that's it."

He paused. "You'd be surprised at how many visitors we get who think that Chianti is only one wine or that there is only one Montepulciano. You'd be astonished. Educated people too. What do they teach them in British schools; in American schools?"

Paul tried not to smile. "I suppose there are other things . . ."

Tonio did not let Paul finish. "And you'd think the French would know better," he continued. "But you'd be wrong if you thought that. They think that there's only one sort of wine—French wine. They don't quite believe that anybody else can make wine. Bordeaux, Bordeaux, Bordeaux. *Toujours Bordeaux*. Heaven knows where people get their ideas from."

"Oh well . . ."

But Tonio was in full flight. "This Chianti business," he continued. "People see a label with *Chianti* printed on it and they think that's a single wine, but the zone of production is vast. Vast. And there are hundreds of different sorts of Chianti."

Paul managed to mention the black cockerel. "I think people recognise the black cockerel symbol. They know about that."

Tonio shrugged. "Maybe, some will, but they are few and far between. And then, of course, there's Lambrusco. The stuff they sell in your supermarkets that calls itself Lambrusco is a disgrace!"

Paul agreed. "Horrible," he said.

"Red lemonade—that's what it is," Tonio went on. "So people think that all Lambrusco is like that—sweet and fizzy—mouthwash, really. And yet there is good Lambrusco—wine that they're proud of up in Modena, Parma, places like that.

The problem is that the big wine growers ferment their wine sweet; they add grape must. Real Lambrusco can be nice and dry—with just a hint of strawberries."

"I've tasted it," said Paul.

Tonio looked at him with new respect. "So you know what I'm talking about."

Paul nodded.

"We have remarkable wines in Italy," said Tonio. "Think of them, those wonderful big red wines from the south—the Sicilian wines that taste of Etna. When I have a glass of one of those in my hand, I close my eyes and I see the volcano smoking."

Tonio's words triggered a memory, and Paul saw it too. The volcano with a puff of white against the deep blue of the Sicilian sky; the rich lava-earth, spewed from the crater, eruptions ago; the green of the vines against the black of the soil. "When I was a boy," he said, "I had a teacher who made us learn poems off by heart."

"I had one too," said Tonio. "Dante. We learned Dante."

"There was a poem by an English writer called Lawrence. D. H. Lawrence. He liked Italy."

"Your English writers did. They all loved Italy."

"And he wrote a poem about a snake he saw in Sicily. I can still recite it. It may sound strange in Italian—or different, at least—but it was about a snake who came to his water trough in the morning. *On a hot, hot day, and I in my pyjamas for the heat* . . . The snake was there before him, you see, and he had to wait. He tells us it was brown, earth-golden, *on the day of Sicilian July, with Etna smoking.*"

Tonio was watching him. "It's good to be able to recite poetry."

"*With Etna smoking* . . . It's always stuck in my mind."

"Like the taste of a wine you love. Like that?"

Tonio did not wait for an answer. "Yes," he continued. "There are so many wonderful wines—some of them not at all well known. Have you ever come across Sardinian Vernaccia? It's very different from our own San Gimignano Vernaccia. It's a bit like sherry and you drink it with *bottarga*. That's grey mullet roe. Very special. But the list goes on and on, my dear friend. Two thousand sorts of wine, I think. Two thousand!"

"That's a very tall tree to be at the top of."

Tonio's eyes narrowed. "Yes, I suppose it is. And we're up there, right at the top, with . . ."

Paul took it as his chance to interrupt. "Barbaresco and Barolo?"

Tonio weighed this suggestion. "Many would say that, yes. If it's Brunello you're referring to."

"Yes, that's what I meant. But why Brunello? Why do you—I mean you personally—think it's so exceptional?"

"Taste," said Tonio. "If you want a simple answer: taste. It tastes good. It was simply a brilliant invention. You know about Ferruccio Biondi Santi?"

"Of course."

Tonio smiled. "They genuflect at his name round here. And I suppose he deserves it. We need our saints, don't we? All of us, whatever we do, we need to have some saints—people who are the heroes of whatever it is we believe in. Religion. Food. Football. Whatever. There have to be saints."

Paul waited for him to continue. He was aware of the fact that he had misjudged Tonio at the beginning. He had come here thinking he would meet a buffoon, and he had met an intelligent and rather appealing man. And yet, although his host had warmed to the discussion of wine, his air of disappointment lingered.

Tonio turned back to the cask and tapped it gently with his knuckles. "Back then in the nineteenth century, Biondi Santi had the great idea of not mixing the sangiovese with other grapes. He left it in the cask for longer than normal. And that made Brunello."

"But there must have been other factors."

"Of course there were. The position. The slopes around Montalcino are perfect for grapes. There is all the sun they need, and yet at night it becomes cool because of the height. That's very good for the acidity. And our soil too, I suppose. Put it all together and you get Brunello. That lovely taste—and the ability to age. That's balance, of course. The wine must have the balance to age for years and years." He paused. "Have you tasted any of the great vintages?"

"They're a bit expensive for me," said Paul.

Tonio shrugged. "The market controls our pleasures, doesn't it? But some of the more recent ones are not too bad—not by the standards of Bordeaux: 2001 was good; 1995 too; 1961."

"I shall just imagine them. There's pleasure in imagining these things."

"Nineteen forty-five," said Tonio. "That was a great vintage, you know. Just think of how bad things were in Italy then. The poverty. The sheer hardship involved in just existing after the War. And Mother Earth comes up with a great gift—a great harvest. She says to Italy, *You've not been very good, you know, and maybe you don't deserve a great vintage—but here it is.*"

"Perhaps she doesn't judge."

"Perhaps not." Tonio glanced at him. "We have a lot to be ashamed of in that period, you know. We try to make out we were victims, but we weren't. We let it happen. We created Mussolini. And many, many families had their Fascists. Mine included."

Paul remembered what Ella had said about Tonio's family. He was about to say something about the past, and the point at which we could detach ourselves from it, when Tonio continued: "My great-uncle was an enthusiastic Fascist," he said. "I am ashamed of that. I am very ashamed." He hesitated. "But everyone has somebody in their family of whom they are ashamed. There cannot be a family anywhere without a skeleton in the cupboard."

Paul thought about this. Tonio was right, he suspected. "We had a fraudster," he said. "A cousin of my father. He defrauded people, then ran off to Australia. He died in a flood in Queensland. He was swept away."

"Well, there you are," said Tonio. "But I must let you taste my wine—rather than just talking about it." He smiled, and beckoned to Paul to join him beside the cask. "We could talk for hours, I think, and be very thirsty at the end of our conversation."

He eased a bung out of the top of one of the casks and inserted a pipette. The wine drawn off was then released into two glasses. Tonio handed one to Paul.

"Rosso di Montalcino," he said. "Here, taste that."

Paul raised the glass to the light. "A very good colour," he said.

"Of course," said Tonio.

Paul sniffed at the glass. "And a fine nose too."

"Very fine," said Tonio, sniffing too.

Paul put the rim of the glass to his lips and took a sip. He rolled the wine round his mouth, drawing air past the liquid. Then he turned to Tonio.

"This is very good," he said.

This brought a beam of pleasure. "Yes, it is, isn't it? Sangiovese grapes—same as those used to make Brunello. Pure sangiovese—nothing added—unlike some, I have never added anything else. And . . ." He paused to give greater weight to his words. "You'll remember how they changed the rules a little while back and allowed Brunello to be sold after twenty-four months in the cask? They allowed Rosso to be sold after twelve months—well, I stick to the twenty-four months. But even with one hundred per cent sangiovese and twenty-four months in the cask, I cannot make Brunello. I have to call my wine Rosso di Montalcino—just because I'm five hundred metres outside the zone of production. Five hundred metres! The man who trims my vines can spit that far!"

"It must be hard for you," said Paul. "This certainly tastes like Brunello. I, for one, could be fooled."

Tonio sighed. "It would be easy for them to redraw the boundaries of the zone of production, but will they do it? They will not. I have asked them time and time again, but they simply say that the zone of production has been fixed and it is impossible to extend it. I ask you!"

Paul made a sympathetic gesture. There was always injustice in any border, in anything. You drew a line and there was always somebody just on the other side; on one side of an arbitrary line there could be happiness and prosperity, on the other misery. But he did not say this.

They continued their tour. Walking up to the vines, Paul looked back over the roof of the house and the *cantina* towards Sant'Angelo in Colle. The scene was one of perfect agricultural simplicity, unchanged, he imagined, from what would have greeted any walker on that path fifty or one hundred years ago. He glanced at Tonio and asked him about the number of cases he sold each year. Tonio gave him the figures. Above them a swallow shot across the sky, dipping and twisting in pursuit of invisible prey. Tonio looked up.

"Swallows," he said.

"Yes," said Paul.

He expected something more, but the other man seemed lost in thought.

"I could have had a very different life," said Tonio suddenly. "I could have lived in Florence or even Milan. I could have lived with people who understood, instead of which I am here, in this place, where I have only the company of people who look down on me."

Paul frowned. "Surely they don't."

"Oh yes, they do," said Tonio. "It is because I only produce Rosso di Montalcino. Many of them condescend to me."

"I don't think they do," said Paul.

"You're kind to say that," said Tonio. "But the truth of the matter is that people who make mere Rosso di Montalcino are largely ignored. Everyone thinks only of their wine— their Brunello."

Paul found it difficult to decide what to say. "You have the consolation of knowing that you make good wine," he said. "That's important in this life, don't you think? If you know you do something well, then it doesn't matter what others think."

This seemed to cheer Tonio up. "You're so right," he said. "That is why the artist will always be happy—no matter how the world treats him. If he knows that what he creates is good, then he can bear the indifference of others."

Their inspection of the vines did not last long. The grapes

were ripening well, said Tonio, and he expected a good harvest. He had a family from Buonconvento who always came to pick for him—solid, reliable people, he said, who had provided sons for the Italian Army for years.

They returned to the house. Tonio announced that he had cooked lunch himself and had made a special effort, as he had heard from his cousin that Paul wrote on food as well as on wine. Paul found himself wondering whether Tonio had a wife; nothing had been said about this, and he had seen no sign of a feminine presence in the house so far. He decided to ask.

"Will we be joined for lunch?" he enquired, as his host served him a small glass of his wine. He had asked for a small glass as he remembered the bulldozer outside. If it was socially irresponsible to drive a car after wine, then how much worse would it be to be in an unfit state in control of a bulldozer. He would ration himself, he decided: one glass on a stomach soon to be filled with a heavy Tuscan lunch would be perfectly safe.

Tonio frowned at the question, and Paul wondered whether he had given offence. But when Tonio answered, he gave no sign of finding the question untoward.

"I am by myself," he said. "I was married—once, but that was some time ago."

"Oh, I see."

"My wife went off with a communist," said Tonio, losing his earlier cheerfulness. "It wasn't easy for me."

"No, of course not . . . I'm sorry."

Tonio acknowledged Paul's sympathy. "It could happen to anyone, you know."

Paul hesitated. His sympathy for Tonio had been building

up. *Poor Tonio,* as Ella had said; he could see now why she called him that. He would confess that he was in the same position—or almost. "My girlfriend—well, she was more than that, really—we had lived together for some time . . ."

"Your mistress?"

"Well, I wouldn't call her that. And I certainly don't think she would. But anyway, she went off. In her case it was with her personal trainer."

Tonio shook his head. "That is very shocking. A personal trainer, you say?"

Paul nodded. "A very fit man."

"We poor men," said Tonio. "We're treated very badly by women, I think. We do our best, but we cannot seem to do anything right."

Paul took a sip of his wine. He would try to cheer things up a bit. "Of course, there are other women. You might meet somebody—you never know."

Tonio looked at him incredulously. "Whom am I going to meet?"

"Well, you never know . . ."

Tonio interrupted him. "I very rarely get invited anywhere."

Paul persisted. "But you never know. If you ask people where they met their wives or partners or whatever, they'll often say they just bumped into them." He paused. "Perhaps you could join something. If you joined an organisation of some sort, then you might meet somebody."

Tonio thought for a moment. "But no organisation has asked me to join them."

"Perhaps you have to ask yourself. What about . . ." He tried to think of something. He knew that the Italians were keen on tennis. There were tennis clubs all over the place, and he had seen one, he seemed to recollect, just outside Montalcino. "What about a tennis club?"

A shadow seemed to pass over Tonio's face. "I don't play."

"But you don't have to be a player to join a tennis club. You can join as a spectator. I'm sure plenty of people do that."

"No, I doubt if they'd want me."

Paul bit his lip. This was discouraging. "Well, there are plenty of other things. What about Internet dating? Plenty of people meet other people that way these days. It's quite standard, you know—at least where I come from. I'm sure Italy's the same."

Tonio looked dubious. "I'm not very good with computers."

"But do you have a friend with a teenage son? They're the experts in working computers. He could get you online."

Tonio looked sad. "All very unlikely," he said.

It seemed to Paul that Tonio's animation and enthusiasm had been replaced by the earlier air of slight sadness. Now he invited Paul into the dining room. Seating his guest at one end of the table, he retreated into the kitchen to retrieve the first course—a Tuscan bean soup. There then followed a pasta course, heavily flavoured with garlic.

This soup was straightforward Tuscan fare, but a perfect illustration, Paul thought, of the merits of simple recipes. The key, he imagined, was the stock.

"Your stock?" he asked.

"Not necessary," said Tonio. "Traditional Tuscan bean soup has only white beans, parsley, garlic and olive oil. We use water. With us, the really important thing is the beans." He paused. "Do you know that famous painting of the bean eater? By Annibale Carracci. It's in Rome somewhere. I have a picture of it in one of my recipe books."

Paul shook his head.

"He sits at the table," said Tonio, "with a spoonful of beans poised to go into his mouth and a plateful in front of him. He has a rather sharp face, our bean eater, but his look of anticipation is very striking. He's really looking forward to his beans."

Tonio tasted the soup. "Yes," he said. "My own garlic. You can never eat enough garlic, you know."

"Keeps vampires away," said Paul.

"Keeps *people* away," muttered Tonio, and then laughed at his own joke.

The next course was wild boar served with fennel.

"Wild boars can be very dangerous," announced Tonio from his end of the table.

Paul had heard a great deal about wild boars, but had seen no sign of them. "I imagine they are," he said. "Do you have many on your property?"

"No," said Tonio. "This was the only one. Now there are none."

Paul looked at his plate. He felt bad about eating it now; it was almost as if he were eating the last of a species, a dodo, perhaps, or an impossibly rare antelope.

Very little was said for the rest of the lunch. At the end of the meal, Paul thanked Tonio for his hospitality and explained that it was time for him to return to the village.

Tonio's mood seemed to have picked up again. "I hope you'll come back," he said. "I've enjoyed your visit."

As he led him to the door, Tonio mentioned that he had a brother in the village. "He's the priest," he said. "He is my younger brother, and a very interesting man he is—very well educated; he was at the Gregorian in Rome, you know. I'm sure you'll meet him. He often goes to the Fiaschetteria Italiana. You must know that place."

"I do," said Paul. "I shall look out for him."

"He is called Stefano," said Tonio.

They went outside. Tonio escorted Paul to the bulldozer and watched, smiling, as he climbed into the cabin.

"Perhaps you'll fix my road on your way out," shouted Tonio, as Paul started the engine.

Paul laughed. "Stranger things have happened," he shouted back. *"Arrivederci!"*

"Ciao!" shouted Tonio, waving. *"Ciao, ciao!"*

Paul looked over his shoulder as he moved off, and saw Tonio standing there, his arm half-raised in a wave, an isolated figure, he thought—a man wanting something that he could never have.

*H*e was becoming accustomed to the bulldozer and its ways by now—so much so that he did not mind its slow pace or the throaty noise made by its diesel engine. The edge was off the afternoon sun, and a pleasantly cool breeze had blown up from the west. He was in no hurry to get back to Montalcino, and when he came to an unmarked turn-off, an unpaved road that dropped down to a small valley, he decided that he would make a brief detour. He suspected that this side-road made a loop and then rejoined the main road back into the village—he had looked at a map and thought he had seen it. He had not explored in this direction before, and he had the time; he might even park the bulldozer and go for a walk if he found a suitable path.

Heavy rain earlier on in the summer had created corrugations in the surface of the road to the extent that in places the verge had been eroded. In a car it would have been an uncomfortable ride, in parts requiring some caution, but on the bulldozer he felt complete confidence. Untidy woodland bordered the road on either side, with patches of scrub bush and, here and there, small, stony fields that had been cleared a long time ago and ignored for years. Many of the trees were young oaks, but a number of trees were far older and provided pools of shade. He passed a farmyard set back from the edge of the road—a rambling house with dark windows like watching eyes, a barn in the entrance to which a cart appeared to have been abandoned, a shed with a door hanging at an angle. Beside the shed, immobile in the shade of a spreading oak, a pair of white Chianina oxen were tethered to a feeding trough. The heads of the oxen drooped, their unnaturally large ears flopping across their brows, only the slow twitching of their tails showing that they were awake, or even alive.

He slowed down as he passed the farmyard, and wondered what it would be like to live in such a place, well out of the village, with no neighbours, and with only olive trees and vines to worry about, and perhaps the oxen and the few sheep that might graze the stony fields. People had lived in that spot, he imagined—in that very house—for centuries. They had survived the conflict of warring principalities, invasion, the heartlessness of landlords, Fascism; they would have been as indifferent to all of these as the countrymen, the *contadini*, always were to the perturbations of the outside world. What would have counted were things far more elemental: the spring rain, the winter frost, fire, the failure of crops. That is what mattered.

For some reason he did not quite understand, he was suddenly gloriously, almost deliriously, happy. It was a physical sensation as much as an emotional one, and he felt as if he were suddenly lighter—able, if he wished, to float upwards and look down on the track, the trees, the farmhouse, the cluttered yard. It was a form of intoxication, a relief from self, a feeling of a sort to accompany being picked up by the wind and effortlessly borne away to a place that it alone decided.

He closed his eyes momentarily, and the wave of elation died away. Opening them in time to prevent the bulldozer wandering off onto the verge, it occurred to him that he felt so happy simply because it was right for him to be here, under this sky, embraced by this warm and scented air, with this hillside slowly rising before him. There was no traffic, no bustle of commerce, nothing in any way redolent of the sleepless hive that cities have become; there was no sense that if human activity suddenly ceased, then everything would clog up and collapse.

He steered the bulldozer round an approaching corner. As he did so, he saw that not far ahead of him a car had left the road and landed in the ditch alongside it. The small red car was nose down, its rear in the air, its back wheels clear of the ground and undergrowth. The front door on the driver's side was open, and he was at once certain that there was a person still inside who, as he approached, stepped out onto the road ahead of him. It was a woman, and she was waving at him.

He brought the bulldozer to a halt, switched off the engine, and climbed out of the cab.

"Are you all right?"

The woman took a few steps towards him. She seemed unharmed, and soon confirmed this.

"Yes, I'm perfectly all right. This all happened in . . ."

Her Italian was correct, but hesitant, and Paul finished her sentence for her in English: ". . . in slow motion?"

She smiled. "Exactly. May we carry on in English?"

"Of course."

He took in the details of her appearance: the casual but expensive clothes; the shoes, with their neat leather tassels; the overall good taste. She was about his age, he thought—perhaps slightly less—and judging from her accent she was American, or, of course, Canadian. She was typical, he thought, of the sort of North American visitor who ventured away from the usual haunts of Florence or Siena, out into Tuscany—there for a reason. He noticed the high cheekbones and the delicate features—an intelligent face.

"I think I might have dropped off," she said. "I don't know otherwise why I should go off the road like that. It just . . . just suddenly happened."

"You went to sleep?"

There was no note of reproach in his tone, but when she replied it was apologetically. "I'm afraid so. I remember feeling tired—I've just arrived, you see, and I've driven up from Rome. I was on the wrong road for ages. All my fault."

He sought to reassure her. "No damage done—that's the important thing."

She gestured to the car. "Except for this."

He glanced at the car. "Rented?"

She bit her lip. "Borrowed."

Paul wanted to smile, not from *Schadenfreude* but out of sympathy, because he could imagine the embarrassment. *That car you lent me—well, there was a ditch, you see, and . . .*

"Oh dear."

She nodded. "Yes." She looked at him helplessly. "What do I do now?"

He moved over to her car and peered through the rear window. Luggage and personal effects were strewn across the seat—a suitcase, an airport bag, a couple of bottles of water, books. He turned to her. "I could try to pull you out."

She glanced at the bulldozer. "With your . . . with that?"

"With my bulldozer—yes. There's a rope. I even seem to have a chain in the back of that thing."

Her relief was evident. "It would be very kind of you." She paused. "I must be holding you back from your work."

Paul shook his head. "No, I was just driving back to Montalcino. I opted for the scenic route—this road doesn't really go anywhere very much."

She explained that she had been making for Montalcino too, but had taken the wrong turning. At the end of her explanation she asked him why he was driving a bulldozer. Did he live nearby? Was he building something?

He met her gaze. "Actually, if I tell you—will you laugh?"

She seemed surprised. "Of course I won't laugh. Why should I?"

"Because people don't drive around on hired bulldozers—or not normally."

She conceded this. "Maybe not." She added, "And I suppose they normally don't go to sleep at the wheel and drive a borrowed car into a ditch."

"Possibly not."

She grinned, and he was struck by the way her face lit up. He liked her. "But rather than standing round talking about bulldozers," he said, "I'm going to get that rope out and see what I can do."

It did not take him long to tie the rope round the blade of the bulldozer and then fix it to the upended rear of her car. Then, while she stood nervously to the side, he started the bulldozer, engaged the reverse gear, and disengaged the clutch. He had intended to move slowly, but his unfamiliarity with reverse meant that he moved faster than he had anticipated. This led to the car being dragged out of the ditch with some suddenness. There was dust and a wrenching, and what sounded to him like the groaning of metal. He stopped, wincing at the violence with which the car had been plucked from its resting place.

Getting out of the cab, he strode over to the car to inspect the damage. The bumper to which he had attached the rope had been bent, but otherwise the car looked unharmed. He turned to her apologetically. "I didn't mean to force it," he said.

She showed no sign of reproach. "But you had to," she said. "And you've done it. You've got me out of the ditch."

"Well . . ."

She was already getting into the driver's seat. "I'll see if it starts."

The car's engine sprang into life, and, leaving it running, she leapt out, took the few steps to where he was standing, and kissed him on the cheek.

"You hero," she said.

He blushed, and she drew back. "I haven't even given you my name," she said. "And yet I'm showering you with kisses. I'm Anna."

"And I'm Paul." He pointed to the car. "Just give it a try. Drive over to the other side of the road. See if everything works."

She got back in and took control. The car moved forward, but with a screeching sound. Applying the brakes, she opened the door and looked anxiously at Paul. He came over, took her place at the wheel, and engaged the gears once more. As the car inched forward, he realised that there was something wrong with the steering, which was stiff and unresponsive. And then the engine stopped.

He tried the ignition again, but with no result. He looked at her and shrugged. "I'm sorry," he said. "It must have taken more of a hammering than we thought. The steering's not working and the engine too . . . It looks like you're going to have to be towed."

She had buried her head in her hands. "This is ghastly," she said. "The car belongs to a friend who's been staying in Rome. She's in Paris for a few months, and she said I could borrow it when I came over. Now I've wrecked it . . ."

"It can be fixed. They can fix these things."

She seemed to take no comfort in his words. "I don't know what to do." Her voice was unsteady. Paul thought she was about to cry; he saw that characteristic moistening of the eyes, the subtle changes that came with the motility of the face.

"Look," he said. "I'll move the car to the side of the road. We can leave it there quite safely. Then you can ride with me into Montalcino—I know where the garage is. We can get them to bring their tow truck out here and pick it up."

Her voice became steadier. "You make it sound so simple."

"Well, it is." He gestured to the back of the car. "Shall I help you with your things? There's plenty of room for your stuff in the cab up there."

After they had cleared the car of her possessions, Paul used the bulldozer to push the car gently to the side of the road. Once it was positioned safely, and with Anna beside him in the cab, he resumed the journey back to Montalcino. On the way, she told him why she was there. "I've come to spend a month here," she said. "It's a complicated story, but I'm writing a book."

"Me too," he exclaimed, and then laughed. "It's a great place to write a book. What's yours about?"

It seemed that she thought he was laughing at her—that he thought her pretentious. She looked away, embarrassed. "Some paintings."

Paul frowned. "I'm sorry—I wasn't being flippant. I'm doing exactly the same thing. I'm writing a book. So when I asked you about yours . . ."

She looked back at him. "It's just that it sounds a bit boastful to tell somebody you're writing a book."

"Books have to be written by somebody. And anyway, tell me about these paintings. I don't think there are many in Montalcino."

"No, I know that. I need to use a library in Siena. But I couldn't face the prospect of a whole month down there. You know how hot it gets. And crowded too."

"So you decided to stay in the hills?"

"Yes."

"And go down there from time to time to the library?"

She smiled. "Yes, that's the plan. Siena for a few days, then back here."

"A good plan, if you ask me."

She became more expansive. "There's an institute in Siena. It's part of the university. They have a collection of materials I'm interested in." She looked at him inquisitively. "But what about you?"

"I'm finishing off some work. It's a book too."

"I really only need a week or so to get through my work," she confessed. "But I'm taking a whole month." She paused. "You haven't told me what you do."

What do I do? thought Paul. He found that he wanted to describe himself in such a way as to impress her, but calling himself a cookery writer made him feel . . . well, less impressive than somebody who wrote on art history.

"I write about food and wine," he said. It sounded so prosaic.

She turned and looked at him with admiration. "Really?"

Paul felt his confidence return. "Yes. I'm writing a book about Tuscan wine and cuisine."

"Oh my God!"

He looked at her in alarm. "What? Something wrong?"

"I know who you are," she said. "I've seen one of your books. *Tables in Bordeaux*, right?"

He felt a flush of pride as he gave the title. *"Paul Stuart's Bordeaux Table."*

"Yes, that's it. I was in Oxford, you see, for two summers. I saw your books in Blackwell's—you know that place. You were there on the tables. I used to see them. I saw your photograph and I thought . . ." She broke off. She had said too much. "You're famous."

Paul smiled. "Hardly."

"But you are."

"No, I'm not. You only get really famous doing the sort of thing I do when you have a television series. I've never had that." He wanted to change the subject, to steer the conversation away from himself.

"What were you doing in Oxford?" he asked.

"I had a visiting fellowship at a college." She seemed embarrassed to be telling him this. Privilege, he thought; it was just too privileged. He had noticed that academics often apologised for their life, for its freedom, for the tenure they enjoyed. And what could be more suggestive of all that than a fellowship of an Oxford college?

"It was a modern one," she said. "It wasn't All Souls, or anything like that. I had a very ordinary office."

He smiled. "I wasn't imagining otherwise."

"It's just that sometimes people think . . . well, they think that if you work in a university you have a better deal than everybody else."

"Don't you?"

Her dismay, written on her face, made him regret his remark. "I'm sorry . . . I didn't mean that to sound the way it did."

She hesitated, but then went on: "My job, you see, is in Massachusetts. I teach at a college there. But they like us to participate in the college's study-abroad scheme. We teach our students during the summer when they're over in places like Oxford and Cambridge. We've also run a summer school in Rome, and Vienna, although I've never been there. I go to the other places regularly because all the students want to do my subject—history of art."

"Hence Siena?"

"Yes. Florentine and Sienese art are my specialties."

"Nice job." He knew, as soon as he said this, that his remark sounded trite, but she appeared not to notice, or at least to mind. She was gazing out of the window. Montalcino could be seen quite clearly now.

"That's it?" she asked.

He felt an almost proprietary satisfaction; the pride of one who, though every bit as much an outsider as those who come later, was there first. "That's the place."

"I love it already."

He stopped the bulldozer so that they could take in the view. From where they were, they could see the Rocca, the pentagonal castle, with its protruding towers. It was too squat to be beautiful, but it acted nonetheless as a fitting backdrop to a stand of Italian stone pines, old and hence large enough to be like great green lollipops planted in the ground. And then, in the curve of the town, there was the wall, describing a lazy parabola around the cluster of buildings that made up the old Montalcino.

"That tower?" she asked.

"The bell tower of the Palazzo dei Priori. It's right in the middle of town. It's a narrow building, as if it were sandwiched between two sets of broader shoulders."

"With bells?"

"With bells. And a clock."

He pointed out the roofs. "You mostly see roofs. The streets are very narrow—so the houses are hidden away. It's a place you only discover once you get into it."

He noticed her expression of delight.

"Happy?" he asked. "The right place?"

"Ecstatic." She looked up at the sky. "It's the same sky as ours, isn't it?"

"In what sense?"

"In the sense that there are no boundaries in the sky. Only air lies between one place in the sky and another place—no matter how far away. Just air."

"I suppose you're right." He wondered what that meant. That we were joined in more ways than we imagined?

"And yet it's so different," she continued. "Our sky where I live is criss-crossed by vapour trails. It has these great white lines drawn across it—as if somebody were parcelling it out. Here . . . well, I don't see a single vapour trail. Just blue."

He looked up. He had heard a plane earlier that day—a distant but insistent droning—but it must have been something smaller, too insignificant to leave a trail.

"Poussin," she said. "You know his skies?"

He tried to remember what Poussins he knew. There was *Landscape with a Man Killed by a Snake;* there was *A Dance to the Music of Time.* That one was full of the cloud on which Time's Chariot was borne. He vaguely remembered the skies; the blue dotted with puffed white cumulus. "I think I can see them," he said.

"These skies are like that. It's the same blue."

"Yes, I suppose it is."

She looked back at him. "And those trees over there, in front of the castle; they look as if they've been placed there by an artist. An artist must have looked at the scene and said, *Trees are needed to complete the picture: here, here and here.*"

He told her that he knew what she meant. The Italian landscape had been inspired by the artistic imagination—not just inspired it.

He asked her where she was staying.

"I've rented a flat for the four weeks I'm here. It's part of somebody's house, I think, but it has a separate kitchen and so on. Just a few rooms. It's not cheap."

He nodded. "It wouldn't be. Brunello has made this place fashionable."

"Such a pity."

He thought about this. "I suppose we have to be careful not to want the places we like to be . . . well, to stay as they were."

He could see that she was expecting him to say more.

"Prosperity changes places—and people too. We can't expect them to stay unspoiled."

"Can't we? Even if they're going to be no happier when they have money?"

"Even then." He had not articulated his ideas on this subject before, but he was sure that he was right. "You can't expect people to choose poverty because it's picturesque." Before Brunello, the people of Montalcino had scratched a living; had they been happier? No. Until recently land had been held at the whim of landlords who kept their tenantry in poverty. That had gone, and the *contadini* no longer had to work for the benefit of rapacious landowners.

She looked chastened. "I'm sorry," she said. "I shouldn't have said what I said. People who have enough to eat shouldn't say that other people looked better when they were thinner."

"That's a neat way of putting it," he said. And as he said this, he thought, *Why did Becky never say anything half as interesting as that?* The thought made him feel guilty: you should not disparage the intellectual ability of your former girlfriends, even if they went off with their personal trainers.

She gave him an enquiring glance. "What are you smiling at?"

"Something I was thinking."

"Something I said?"

He shook his head. "No, I was thinking of one of those odd rules of life—you know, things you shouldn't do."

"And did you ever do it—this thing you shouldn't do?"

"I did it just then," he said. "But then I realised I shouldn't and I thought of something else." He changed the subject. "See that church?" he said. "It's called the Chiesa della Madonna del Soccorso."

She looked up. "Do you believe in her?" she asked.

"The Virgin Mary?"

"Yes."

"No," he said. "Not at all. She's a Mediterranean goddess, don't you think? Absorbed lock, stock, and barrel into Christianity."

"Maybe. But aren't you being a bit harsh? Shouldn't people be allowed their scraps of comfort?"

"Am I being harsh? Yes, perhaps I am." He paused. "Do you believe in her?"

"I like the thought of her. She's Mother, isn't she? And I quite like the idea of Mother."

"Your scrap of comfort?"

"Perhaps."

8

Dried Leaves, Blown Seeds,
the Charity of the Winds

The garage was just inside the town walls. The road on
which it stood was barely wide enough to accommodate the
bulldozer, and so Paul returned it to the car park; they would
seek out the mechanic on foot. The notice was still in its
new location, and nobody had attempted to park in the bulldozer's place. Of the attendant there was no sign; she spent
most of her time, he had noticed, at the car park up near the
Rocca, where she could talk to her friends and, he imagined,
do a brisker trade in parking fines.

Anna had managed to cram most of her possessions sal-
vaged from the car into two cases. A few books, though,
would not fit in, and Paul suggested that these could be left
in the bulldozer, even if the cab did not lock securely.

He picked up a dark-covered paperback and read the title.
"I don't think anybody is going to steal *Caravaggio: A Life*," he
said. He put it down and picked up another one. "Or *Il Rina-
scimento a Mantova,* for that matter."

She laughed. "I would."

He looked askance. "Steal from a bulldozer?"

"No, not really. It was a joke."

"They'll be quite safe. I'll fetch them for you later." He
began to tuck the books away in the compartment where he
had found the tow rope, but lingered over *Caravaggio*.

"Do you like his work?" asked Anna.

"Caravaggio?"

She was watching him, and he felt that he was being assessed. But she was a teacher, after all, he told himself, and teachers assessed . . .

He flicked through the book once more, which fell open at a sumptuous picture of four young musicians.

"I've seen that," he said. "Not in the original, but a print of it."

She looked over his shoulder. "He painted that for a patron. For Cardinal del Monte. He spent some time in the Cardinal's house in Rome. He painted several pictures for him."

Paul remembered something about Caravaggio. "But wasn't Caravaggio a bit . . . a bit wild? Was he a good guest at the Cardinal's?"

She thought for a moment. "The Cardinal liked a party. He had day-long concerts. Banquets too."

"Ah."

"But you're right about Caravaggio's bad behaviour. You probably know he had to flee Rome because he'd killed somebody." She paused, and looked at him. He noticed, for the first time, the colour of her eyes—a flecked green. "People said that it was an argument over a game of tennis. But there's a theory now that it was an argument with a rival over a woman. Or a boy. It could have been either with Caravaggio, I suspect."

His eyes went to the picture once more. The musicians were young men, and there was an erotic charge in their gaze from the canvas. They were dangerous.

Anna stepped down from the bulldozer and Paul passed her the cases. "It's not all that far," he said. "But if you like, I can go and find the village taxi. You could wait here with the cases."

She shook her head. "I'll manage." And then she added, "I've ruined your day, you know. There you were, driving along on your . . ."

"My bulldozer."

"Yes, on your lovely Italian bulldozer and you meet me. And I make you carry a suitcase all over the place, and all the time you should be doing whatever it is you have to do."

"Eat. Drink."

"Well, that's your job, isn't it?"

He laughed, and picked up both cases. "I can carry both— I'll be balanced that way. Yes, it is my job, but I don't do it all the time. I'm also a driver and a porter, as it happens. So let's go."

It did not take long to reach the garage, where the mechanic, a short man in blue overalls and with grey, frizzy hair, emerged from under a car to hear Paul's account of what had happened. Anna remained silent, but followed the conversation with interest. From time to time the mechanic looked at her, as if to obtain confirmation. As he listened he wiped his hands on a piece of blue cloth.

"That's an issue with that make of car," he pronounced at last. "The steering . . ." He made a dismissive sound with his lips.

"You'll be able to fix it?" asked Paul.

The mechanic sighed. He gestured to a cluster of cars parked untidily behind his garage. "I've got to deal with all of those," he said. "And my assistant has had to go into hospital in Siena. He's having an operation. Here." He pointed to his stomach. "He's going to be off work for a month—during which I'm going to have to pay him, of course."

Anna looked anxiously at Paul. "Tell him it's borrowed from a friend. I have to fix it."

Paul explained, and the mechanic looked sympathetically at Anna. "I can only do what I can do," he said. "And I'll try. I can fetch it this evening. I can get hold of a truck that will . . . you know, pick it up and bring it in." He made a lifting gesture. "But then . . ." He shrugged. "Maybe two or three weeks. It depends on getting the parts. You know how these people are. They have to get them from Turin or somewhere, and then they lose them and you have to reorder them. It can take a long time. You're in their hands, you see."

Paul understood. He had encountered this in Italy on occasion: the conviction that you were at the mercy of somebody else, somewhere distant—in Rome as often as not—who had power over you and who did not have to explain or justify how it was exercised.

"But I'm sure you'll do your best."

The mechanic nodded, and Paul handed over the key. "This lady is very grateful," he said. "It's been a bad day for her."

The mechanic looked at Anna. He managed a smile. "Bad days sometimes end well," he said. "Sometimes." He hesitated, looking at his watch. He asked where they were headed, and Anna gave an address. Paul recognised that this was not far from the hotel.

"I could run you there," said the mechanic. "I have to go that way."

"You're very kind."

The mechanic shrugged. "You've been unfortunate. This is how Italy sometimes welcomes people—with misfortune."

$\mathscr{T}$he small apartment that Anna had rented was a few yards down the hill from the Fiore, so close to the hotel that its windows looked up and into the hotel's dining room. The two buildings were separated only by a strip of garden and an ancient, half-collapsed wall.

"It seems that we're neighbours," said Paul, as he helped Anna with her suitcases. "I'm staying up there—in the Fiore."

They thanked the mechanic, who promised that he would attend to her car as soon as he could, but would phone her, anyway, the following week to let her know of progress. Then together they carried her cases to the door of the house in which she had been told she would find her apartment. A ring of the doorbell produced the landlord, a small, rotund man who beamed a welcome. Yes, he had been expecting her, and yes, the *Professoressa* was very welcome to leave her suitcases in the hall while he showed her to her accommodation, and yes, he thought that she would be very comfortable and would want for nothing.

Anna turned to Paul. "Well, I can't thank you enough."

He made a self-deprecatory gesture. "I couldn't have left you in the ditch." He paused. It was clear that she was keen to settle in and did not want him to linger.

"I was . . ."

She looked at him enquiringly.

"I was wondering whether . . . perhaps . . . we might meet for dinner. Or rather, I could take you out for dinner. There are a few good places."

She looked at him thoughtfully. "I was going to sort things out and . . ."

"Of course not tonight," he said hurriedly. "Tomorrow?"

She hesitated, and then accepted. "Tomorrow . . . yes, all right."

"We could go to the Stracotto," he said. "Do you like mushrooms? They do some amazing things with mushrooms."

She nodded, but she seemed distracted. Her thanks—

effusive and clearly genuinely meant—had been warm enough, but now she seemed slightly cool. She clearly wanted to see her apartment and he was going on about mushrooms. He smiled sheepishly. "Sorry, you have to get on with things and I don't need to tell you about their mushroom risotto."

"No, it doesn't matter."

He laughed nervously. "I've got a lot to say about mushrooms, but I won't bore you." It was an inconsequential thing to say, and he regretted it. *He* was the one who had rescued her; *she* was the newcomer who had very little Italian and who knew nothing of Montalcino, and yet here he was feeling inadequate.

The landlord jingled the keys impatiently, and Paul took his leave. Rather than go back to the Fiore, he decided to drop in on the Fiaschetteria Italiana for a cup of coffee. He felt unsettled; there was elation—she had agreed to have dinner with him—but there was something else, a feeling of doubt, of uncertainty. Her acceptance of his invitation had seemed hesitant. But was that at all surprising? They had met only a couple of hours ago, and he had been driving a bulldozer at the time. What woman would accept an invitation to dinner from somebody who had simply appeared, quite without warning, on a *bulldozer*?

He smiled at the thought. People often judged others by their cars: sporty types drove fast cars, timid types drove modest, under-powered cars, green types drove green cars, and so on. But who drove a bulldozer? He imagined her calling a friend to say, "I've been invited out to dinner with a man who drives a bulldozer." And the friend would have to warn, "Be careful—just be careful. Don't let him push you around . . ."

Or was she married? Or had she a regular boyfriend? He had assumed that there was nobody, but on reflection he realised he had no grounds to make that assumption. It was perfectly possible that she was in some sort of relationship; she was attractive and interesting—why should she not be with somebody who was unable to come with her to Italy because he was working?

He felt embarrassed by his gaucherie. He should have suggested something less significant than dinner—a coffee in the Fiaschetteria, for instance; that would seem less like an actual date. That's what somebody who knew nothing about the circumstances of another should propose—and then use the opportunity to find out whether somebody was single or available. It was a matter of elementary social nous and he had failed to exercise it.

Onesto was in the café, sitting at the table at which they had met before, immersed in a copy of *Corriere della Sera*. As Paul entered, he laid aside his newspaper and gestured for Paul to join him.

"So," he said. "You've been off on your researches. I hear you went out to Tonio's."

Paul was surprised that he should know. Had he said anything to Onesto about it? He did not think so. "You heard?"

"Yes, of course." It was as if it were the most natural thing that he should know. He went on to explain: "People round here—they like to know what's going on, you see." He was watching the effect of his words, and there was a note of satisfaction in his voice. "There are no secrets in Montalcino."

Paul signalled to the waiter. "Scotland is a bit like that—or parts of Scotland."

This seemed to please Onesto. "Perhaps we Italians are a bit like you." He took a sip of his coffee. "And Tonio? What did you think of his place?"

"He gave me a warm welcome," said Paul. "He showed me round. We talked about everything. The wine. The place. His family history."

Onesto put down his coffee with a force that rattled the saucer. "His family history!" he exclaimed. "That nonsense!"

Paul shrugged. "I suppose he's proud of who he is . . ."

Onesto did not let him finish. "Pah!" he spat out. "Pah! Pah!"

Paul studied his companion's expression. The Italian left could express itself forcibly, and of course one might expect a provincial teacher, schooled in the tradition of Gramsci, to have strong views on the vestiges of the aristocracy.

"It's all dreamed up," Onesto continued. "He has no more family history than I do, and I'm as proletarian as they come."

"So he's bogus?"

"Of course he is," said Onesto. "Listen, I like Tonio well enough—I've got nothing against him. But do you know who his people were? A few generations ago they were charcoal burners. They used to live in the woods down near Sant'Antimo—they had a shack down there. Then they rose a bit, but were still *contadini* like the rest of us. Tonio's father had a brother called Ernesto, who had one exceptional talent, and he knew how to use it."

The waiter came to take Paul's order. Before he moved off, Onesto said to him, "Domenico, have you heard this? Our friend here went over to Tonio's place—you know, down near Sant'Angelo, that place, and met His Excellency."

Onesto and the waiter both burst out laughing.

Onesto turned to Paul. "You see?" he said. "Everybody knows that it's nonsense. I don't know how he thinks anybody will be taken in—apart from foreigners. But this Ernesto, you see—Tonio's uncle—he was a very handsome man. Some said the best-looking man in Italy."

"That was the talent you mentioned?"

"Well, being good-looking is not necessarily a talent—but using your looks, now that is a talent, I think." Onesto now gave Paul an apologetic glance. "Ernesto Poggio—that was their family name, by the way—none of this Bartolo del Bosco nonsense—he knew how to get the ladies excited, if you'll forgive the expression. They took one look at him and they became . . . well, quite aroused. Their eyes took on this strange look. It was amazing."

"A great gift," said Paul.

Onesto nodded. "There are many men who would have given everything to have that, but . . ." He broke off, to make one of those Italian gestures that expresses acceptance of the way the world is.

"And so?"

Onesto was gazing across the café, out through the door to the square beyond. The afternoon light was gentler now, and the sky, just visible above the roofline, was taking on the soft tones of evening. "What happened?" he mused. "Ernesto was no slouch: he had a very good look round—went to Siena to see if he could find a wealthy woman down there, but finally decided that the best prospect was right on his doorstep. There was that nice little place down near Sant'Angelo where the owner was getting on a bit—his mind was wandering—and there were no sons to make trouble, just a daughter. Land, you know, means more to these people than anything else. Money in the bank is just money in the bank—land you can touch, you can plant things in it, you can stand on it. That's what they understand. That's the peasant mentality, you see. And so he set to work, and he and this daughter married and that was that. The charcoal burners from Sant'Antimo had done rather well for themselves."

Paul pointed out that things like that happened.

"Of course they do," said Onesto. "But plans can go wrong, can't they? That was back in the late nineteen thirties. Ernesto should have kept his head down—concentrated on improving the place – but he didn't. He became a Fascist—a very prominent, noisy Fascist. And then, when the Germans retreated and the whole thing collapsed, he and his wife were captured by partisans, and I'm afraid that justice was summary in those days—scores had to be settled. They were strung up—upside down, like Mussolini and his mistress—and that was it. That was the end to the uniforms and the high life."

Paul winced. He found it hard to think of Italy as a brutal country—but it had been.

"And so after they had disposed of them, you might have thought that the farm would have been confiscated, but there was too much going on and nobody was interested. There were no children, and so it was taken over by Ernesto's much younger brother, who was not much more than a teenage boy at the time. That was Tonio's father, Alfonso. When he died, Tonio took over. A few years later he changed the family name and started calling himself Bosco. I suppose if you're descended from charcoal burners, then you may as well call yourself wood."

"And the Bartolo?"

Onesto shrugged. "That came out of the air somewhere. He must have come across the name in the newspaper somewhere. There was a famous jurist called Bartolo—if I remember correctly. Down in Perugia, I think. People laughed, but he didn't seem to care, and he even put it on a sign outside the property. Somebody painted inverted commas round the name—you can still see them—but that didn't put Tonio off.

Everybody laughs, of course. They think it's the best joke for a long time. In fact, they'd be disappointed if he started calling himself Poggio. People need somebody to laugh at, don't you think?"

Paul found his sympathy for Tonio was growing. He recalled the rather lonely figure standing there, waving goodbye to him as he drove off on his bulldozer. What would it be like to be an object of ridicule? People survived, as they always did. Social outcasts lived through their oppression, somehow got over the exclusion with which they were visited. He remembered a boy at school, a boy called Macdonald, who had been effeminate in his manner and had been mocked as a result. He remembered a conversation he had had with him when he was nine or ten, and Macdonald had said to him, *I'm not a girl, you know—they call me that, but I'm not, you know.*

He answered Onesto's question. Yes, people needed their targets.

"Not that I laugh at him myself," said Onesto quickly. "As I said, I rather like him. Poor Tonio."

But you did laugh, thought Paul, remembering the exchange with the waiter. But he said nothing about that, and the conversation moved on to what he had been writing.

"This book of yours," said Onesto. "What is it? A book for the kitchen? A cookery book?"

Paul did not want to sound presumptuous, but he was not a writer of cookery books, even if his books did contain at least some recipes. "A bit more than that. It's about food, rather than how to cook it."

Onesto nodded. "Philosophy? That sort of thing?"

Paul felt that he could not dignify his work quite that much. "Only in a very general sense," he said. "I suppose the way that people treat their food is a philosophical question. But it's also an aesthetic question."

Onesto mulled this over. "Like the Futurists?" he asked. "Marinetti and his friends?"

Paul smiled. "They were pretty extreme. And I don't think I'd agree with them, anyway. For one thing, I like pasta."

It was clear that Onesto was pleased that Paul had picked up on his reference. "I used to be interested in Futurism— when I was at college. Futurist literature. Futurist art. I thought it exciting."

Paul agreed. "Well, it must have been. Everything they proposed was against the established order. They stood things on their head, and when you're that age, that can be attractive." He thought of how he had been when he was nineteen. He had looked for something to revolt against, but it had been hard.

Onesto had grinned at the mention of pasta. "They actually argued that pasta made the population lethargic. A heavy, pasta-dominated cuisine created a slow, heavy people; that's why pasta had to go if Italy was to regain her energy."

"Bizarre."

"But not as bizarre as their Futurist banquets," said Onesto. "They went in for strange combinations. Meat and pineapple. Dishes with scents piped over them." He paused, remembering something else. "And they teamed up with the Fascists, who tried to get people off pasta because the wheat had to be imported. Rice was more Italian, they said. More virile and altogether heroic. Anything about that in your book?"

"No," said Paul. "I tend not to write much about new ways of eating."

Onesto was interested. "Why not?"

"Because they don't last," said Paul. "The food people eat

here—anywhere in rural Tuscany, for that matter—is much the same as the food their grandparents ate. The same mushrooms. The same cheeses. The same sauces. These things last. Futurism didn't. The anti-pasta movement didn't get far—the *mangiamaccheroni,* the macaroni eaters, triumphed in the end."

"So they did," said Onesto. "Thank heavens. Perhaps people started to look at the Futurists' manifestos and read their claims that museums and art galleries should be demolished because they glorified the past."

Paul said that it was always a good idea to read any movement's manifesto before supporting it, although few people did. "Politicians rely on that," he said. "They prefer people not to examine Plan A too closely, let alone Plan B."

Onesto picked up his newspaper and glanced at the headlines. Then he made a gesture that Paul was not entirely sure about. He understood the common Italian hand gestures, but this one, a twirling movement followed by a quick flick of the wrists was new to him. *Dialect,* he thought.

After he left the café, Paul decided to walk a complete round of the village before returning to the Fiore. The heat of the day was now almost entirely dissipated, and the air was limpid and cool enough for comfort. The visitors who descended on the village during the day—bus parties from Siena and Florence—had disappeared, and only a few stragglers, who had made their way there by car, remained. He walked along the path on top of the outer town wall until he reached the church. From the churchyard a path descended the hill through an olive grove. On impulse he followed this along the contour of the hillside, reaching at length another, much smaller church, deserted now and overgrown with creepers, its roof collapsed in places, its windows long since stripped of their glass. In the doorway of the church, carved into the stone of the jamb, was a small slot, like a letterbox, above which was incised the word *eleemonsyna*, alms. The letters were worn with the effect of the weather, and the slot itself was blocked with the detritus of the trees above—dried leaves, blown seeds, the charity of the winds.

He touched the stone lettering, and when he looked at the finger with which he had traced the letters, it was brown with dust. Leaning forward, he peered through the split timber of what had once been the heavy wooden door, now thin with rot. He felt the touch of cool air wafted out from the interior of the church—the feeble breath of a dying building.

The growth around the windows, the intrusive ivy, made it dark inside, but as his eyes grew accustomed to the gloom, he was able to make out the shape of old pews, some upended, others still where they would have been before the last congregation deserted. A cupboard stood against the wall, its door open at a drunken angle. And there was the stone altar, covered by the remnants of a cloth, now no more than disjointed fragments, like thick cobwebs.

He drew in his breath sharply. There had been a movement—so quick, so brief he could not make it out, but something had moved. He drew back. It could have been anything—a bird, a bat, perhaps even a cat that had wandered down from the village and become feral. And then he heard it. It was a cough.

Paul turned on instinct and retraced his steps down the path. There had been somebody in the church, and this person, whoever it was, had been aware of his presence. He looked over his shoulder. There was no sign of life, but something made him want to get back up to the village as quickly as he could.

He thought: It could be anything. It could be lovers, disturbed in their meeting place, not expecting that somebody would come and peer through the door. It could have been children—boys finding somewhere secret to carry out their boyish plans. It could have been a hiker who had been attracted to the cool interior of the church to catch up on sleep. It was ridiculous to take fright over what was merely an unexpected human encounter, but the desire to get away had been too strong. He wanted now just to be back within earshot of the village, back in the light, away from this place of ancient stone and shadows.

9

I Have Deleted the Word *Love*

$\mathcal{H}$e did not sleep well. The room had wooden shutters, but even when closed these allowed a chink of light from the street to penetrate the darkness, throwing delicate tracings across the room. At three in the morning he was wide awake, staring up at the patterns of light along the ceiling. He was still unsettled—the feeling of unease he had experienced on his walk had lingered, but now this was mixed with a strange sense of anticipation, an excitement at the prospect of seeing Anna again. He had thought about her frequently since they had parted earlier the previous day. He had gone over in his mind everything she had said about herself. He had pictured again the car and her possessions and the way she had looked at him when they had been travelling together on the bulldozer. He tried to remember the exact colour of her eyes—that green, flecked effect—and the way she held her head. And then he sat up in bed—bolt upright—and thought: *I've fallen for her.*

Paul turned on his light. The finding of a word for an emotion may sometimes help to defuse the emotion, may help to deprive it of its power. If we know we are angry, and find the words to express our anger, our temper abates. If we know we are in love, then that self-knowledge may take the edge off love's itch. But the words themselves—the words we use in our mind—determine the shape of the thought. *I've fallen for her* is different from saying *I'm in love with her.*

He got out of bed and crossed the room to his window. Unlatching the shutters, he looked out into the night, and found his eyes drawn to the house where she was staying. In a room behind one of those windows, *she* was sleeping.

He went back to the other side of the room and flicked the light switch. It took a few moments for his eyes to adjust, but when they did he saw that the night sky was clear. He looked up, losing himself in the blackness and the fields of stars. He could make out a few constellations, but did not know their names, apart from Sagittarius, the Bowman, which he thought he could distinguish. He left the shutters open, enjoying the cool air that now came into the room. He returned to his bed and tried to think of his work. He had to finish the book, and it would not do to become involved in some short-term holiday romance—if she were to be interested, of course, which was by no means clear. What was the point? She would go back to the United States in a few weeks and he to Scotland. There was nothing to be gained by making himself miserable in the way in which sixteen-year-old boys tormented themselves over girls. He was beyond all that. He wanted to settle down. He wanted somebody with whom to have a family. He wanted stability, predictability, and, yes, loyalty—the last of these being something that Becky so obviously did not have. Becky . . . He closed his eyes. He did not want to think about her. The personal trainer was welcome to her. No, he was not. He would take her back if she came to him; he would take her back immediately, and without question. He stopped himself. No, he would not do that. It was just sex that he was thinking of. That was all. There was nothing that he wanted to *say* to Becky, whereas there was so much that he wanted to say to Anna. He wanted to tell her everything.

The sleepless night meant that he was late in waking up, and was disturbed by the sound of the chambermaid vacuuming the corridor outside. The Fiore served a light breakfast, but he had missed that, and so he went instead to the Fiaschetteria, where he read the paper over a steaming cup of coffee and a salami roll. He was beginning to recognise some of the locals now, and even exchanged morning greetings with one or two of the people he saw going about their business in the Piazza del Popolo. Acceptance in a place like Montalcino would come at different levels, and at a different pace depending on what sort of acceptance was involved. To be fully accepted was impossible, unless one were a Montalcinese, born and brought up in one of the villages, and even then there was a deeper form of acceptance that required more than one generation to have lived there. A child born in Montalcino, but to parents from somewhere else, would obviously feel at home, but would never have quite the same entitlement as a child whose grandparents were Montalcinesi. Such a child would always be half something else: half a southerner, half a Roman, half a Florentine.

Day visitors were too numerous and too transitory to have any role, other than a useful economic one, but those who stayed a few days or, even more so, a few weeks would be the object of interest. Paul had already seen that in Onesto's awareness of his visit to Tonio. This interest would be expressed in looks and nods, in the exchange of a few words about the news of the day or the weather, but that would be all. Anything more would require years.

Paul returned to his work after breakfast, and made good progress, in spite of his distraction. By lunchtime, though, he was tired, and took a siesta that became an hour or so of deep sleep. When he woke up, he looked at his watch and worked out that in four hours' time he would be seeing Anna again. He wondered how he would pass the time until then, and decided to make a complete circuit of the village, carefully avoiding the street on which she was staying—he did not want her to think he was looking for her. At the same time, though, he rather hoped that he might meet her; that they might talk for a while and then she might suggest that they should meet a bit early in order to have an aperitif in the Fiaschetteria before going on to the restaurant. But they did not meet, and when he returned to the hotel there were still several hours to wait.

He decided to check his e-mails. He had looked earlier on in the day, when he had switched on his computer, but had not seen anything worth bothering about. There were a few routine matters, but nothing that could not wait for a bit before eliciting a response. But now there was something worth bothering about.

He saw her name at the top of the list of messages. Beside it was a red exclamation mark, signifying urgency. He hesitated; the delete button was only a finger away, and it would be so easy to send the message, unread, into whatever black hole consumed such spurned messages—a vast galactic soup of pharmaceutical offers, enticing news of unexpected and apocryphal legacies, of advance warnings as to the imminent collapse of the world's banking system, of unanswered appeals from forgotten almae matres. But he did not; it occurred to him that Becky might be in some sort of trouble, and his conscience would not allow him to ignore her.

He clicked the message open. *Paul, Hope this finds you well. I know you're in Italy, because Harry told me. I need to talk to*

*you—I really do. I tried your mobile, but it was switched off. Please,
Paul—we really need to talk. I'm coming out to see you. I've booked
my flight, to Rome and will come up to Siena by train. Harry told
me you're staying in a place called Mont-something or other. I made
a note of it. I'll make my own way there—is that OK? I won't stay
long—just three or four days.*

He read the message through with growing despair. Then
he read it again, groaning as he did so. At least try to put her
off, even if he only managed to contact her at the airport.

He found his mobile and brought up her number, although
he could still call it to mind, as he could do with so many
details of their long relationship—her computer password,
the PIN of her bank accounts. These were the equivalent of
the mementoes that in the past lovers kept, preserved and
cherished—folded love letters, locks of hair, dried flowers
pressed between the pages of an album, love tokens of every
sort. There were no flowers or letters any more, just the
telegraphese of electronic mail, the faded leaves of the vir-
tual world. In the delay as the system connected, he thought
of what he would say. He would be kind to her, but he had
to be resolute—that was the only way. If you left the door
open after a split-up, then you would never be able to bring
things to an end. You had to be clear about it; no *ifs* or *buts*—it
was over. And after all, it was not his fault; she had done it;
she was the one who had left—he had no reason to reproach
himself.

He heard a click, and then the announcement that the
number was unavailable. This told him that she had turned
the phone off, and that, in turn, meant that she was somewhere where mobiles were disallowed—a cinema, a concert
hall, an aeroplane . . .

He tried her landline and this time was answered with

a recording inviting him to leave a message. He hesitated before beginning: *It's just me.* (He had always said that to her; another relic of their past together.) *I've had your e-mail and, look, it's not a brilliant idea to come over here. In fact, I would prefer it if you didn't. I don't want to be unfriendly . . . don't think that, but just don't come. Please.* And with that he signed off. Then he wrote a response to her e-mail. *This is not a good idea, Becky. I'm sorry, but I really don't think you should come. I don't want you here—I'm sorry if that sounds unfriendly, but it's the way I feel. So . . . please don't come. Love, Paul.* Going back over it, he deleted the word *Love,* and inserted *Best wishes.* He thought: I have deleted the word *love* . . . it could be the beginning of a poem. It was ready to send, and he did so before he considered any other changes to the wording.

*B*y the time he went to meet Anna, he had recovered his composure. He had decided that the only way in which he could enjoy the evening was to put Becky's message out of his mind. He had always been rather good at suppression—as a young boy, when for several months he had attracted the attention of the school bully, he had succeeded in concealing the fact from his parents by the simple technique of pretending that it was not happening; it was only when his mother noticed the bruises that the matter came to light. He employed the tactic later on, to greater or lesser extent, as a means of denying unpleasant reality, and as a result acquired a reputation for stoicism. Such an approach to life could be problematic, of course, as denial dulls pain even if it fails to remove its causes. But it was useful that evening; Becky might have been imminent, but for the few hours of his date with Anna, she would not succeed in dampening his spirits.

They made their way to the restaurant slowly, aware of

the early evening parade of others around the main piazza and through the town's main street, aware of the fact that they, like everyone else, were being watched.

"*La bella figura,*" said Paul. "That's what this is all about."

Anna had heard the expression, but was not quite sure about it.

"It's at the heart of Italian life," Paul explained. "At the absolute heart. It's about making an impression. It's about doing things beautifully."

"Doing what?"

He gestured towards a couple walking arm in arm about the piazza. "Them, for instance. They're going for a walk before their dinner, but they aren't walking for the sake of walking—not as exercise. They're walking to show off their clothes. They're walking around to show that they know how to behave stylishly. *La bella figura.* And when they get home and she puts the meal on the table, she'll do so with a flourish. More *bella figura.*"

Anna said that it sounded like a whole philosophy of life.

"Yes, it is," said Paul. "Acting with an eye to how things look."

A small flock of pigeons—no more than half a dozen—that had been pecking at something on the road now rose in a flutter to sanctuary on the rooftops.

"Even the pigeons," observed Paul. "Even the way they fly is elegant."

"Come on!"

"No, it's true. I know it sounds ridiculous, but have you ever seen the pigeons in Siena? In that gorgeous shell-shaped piazza? Have you seen them fly up to the bell tower? It's so beautiful—the birds against those red bricks and the sky. *La bella figura.* It's about everything in this country—everything."

"Even driving a bulldozer?"

He laughed. "Even driving a bulldozer . . . You see, if an Italian were to drive a bulldozer, he'd do it much more elegantly than I do—with more panache."

"He'd drive it . . . theatrically?"

It was just the right word. "Yes, theatrically. This whole country is theatrical—even the way bulldozers are driven—it's one great big theatre. And there's a role for everybody—nobody's left out."

A woman walking past them in the opposite direction greeted him formally. For a few moments he did not recognise her, but then, as she went past them, he remembered.

"She knows you?" asked Anna.

"She runs a shop I've been going into," said Paul. "It's an *alimentari*. I went there to buy some grapes and I became rather involved in a discussion about cheese. I see her most days, and she's taken to greeting me in the street."

"I adore cheese," said Anna. "I've already gorged myself. I bought a whole chunk of Parmesan yesterday, and I somehow seem to have got through half of it without really trying."

"It's my favourite too," said Paul. "I know it doesn't sound very imaginative, but I think it's hard to beat Parmesan when it's just the right age. The problem is that many people outside Italy eat it when it's either too young or when it's dried out. Those cartons of Parmesan you used to be able to buy—you know, the ones with the little plastic spouts—I always felt the cheese they contained tasted liked powdered cardboard."

"But there are plenty of others, aren't there? From right around here?"

"Tuscany has its cheeses," said Paul. "Are you adventurous?"

"I like to think I am."

"Then I can ask them in the restaurant to produce some of their *pecorino nero*. We can eat it with honey."

She smiled. "Is that adventurous?"

"*Pecorino nero*'s rare. It's made from the milk of black-fleeced sheep. And it's adventurous because not everybody likes the idea of eating sheep's milk cheese."

"I'm up for it."

"Good. And then there's *pecorino Senese*, which is *pecorino* rubbed in olive oil, tomato paste, and, in the place we're going to, with ashes. We can add honey to the mix if we like."

They reached the restaurant, which was just beginning to get busy. He studied the menu and spotted the wild boar. He asked her whether she had had it before, and she had not. Nor had she tried artichoke soup drizzled with truffle oil.

"I know so little about food," she said. "I eat it, and I cook when I need to, but that's about it." She paused, before adding, "Unlike you."

"I know less than you think," he said modestly. "It's not hard to write a book about food and wine, you know. It's all been written before—somewhere. You just have to know where to find it. Then you dress it up."

She affected shock. "You don't mean you plagiarise?"

"No, I don't mean that. That's the biggest sin in academia, isn't it?"

"Probably," she said. "It's a big problem for students these days because they can't remember where they found the information for their essays. It's all there—all online—they just have to search for it. But even if they take notes—which they do—they may find they're using the words they've read on the screen. Then somebody checks up and finds it's repeated verbatim in their essay. Plagiarism."

"And what about their professors?"

"Do they plagiarise? Is that what you're asking?"

He nodded.

She replied that sometimes they did. And sometimes it was intentional. "If you're a professor without tenure, you're under tremendous pressure to publish. But what if you've got nothing to say?"

"Then perhaps you're in the wrong job."

"Perhaps, but you probably won't think that. And you may be a brilliant teacher, but nobody's going to pay much attention to that. That's not going to get you tenure. You have to show that you're a scholar."

"You're not justifying it, are you?"

She was not. "All I'm saying is that you can see why people do it."

He said that you could say that about anything. "You can see why people steal things. You can see why they commit murder. But I'm not sure if that takes us any further . . ." He suddenly thought of Occhidilupo. Could he see why Occhidilupo was as he was? Of course he could. A mean, brutal upbringing in a desolate southern landscape. A father who was violent in the home, a low-ranking member of the Camorra or the 'Ndrangheta. A conviction, instilled at an early age, that you had to battle for anything you had; needed to fight and bite and scratch to get anywhere, because for most people around you that was exactly what they had to do if they were not to be left to fester where they started. And you could trust nobody, of course, because they were all looking out for themselves and they saw no reason to do anything to help.

The waiter appeared and offered to recite the evening's specials.

"I don't know what to choose," said Anna. "I'd probably order the wrong thing."

He made a few suggestions that she seized upon with relief. Paul ordered sparkling wine for both of them. They touched glasses.

"To the success of your research," he said.

"And yours," she responded.

"In my case, this meal counts as research."

She looked surprised. "You'll write about it?"

"Possibly. We'll see."

He asked her about her plans to get to Siena. "There's a regular bus service," he said, "which would be better—even if you had a car."

"Or a bulldozer?"

"Yes, or a bulldozer."

Then she said, "My friend will have a car."

He had picked up the menu as she spoke. He gazed at it, his eyes unfocused. *Her friend.* "You know somebody here?" he asked, his voice strained.

"No, it's somebody who's coming to see me. In a couple of days' time."

He tried to look unfazed. "Coming from where?"

"From the States. He's only got a week—or slightly over, but the flights will take up a bit of it."

He thought of the straws he might clutch. The friend was a childhood acquaintance—somebody she had kept up with over the years. Or he was the boyfriend of a cousin of hers; the cousin was in Singapore and he was breaking his journey in Italy on his way to see her because he had business in Rome. It was an easy add-on to get up to Tuscany. Or the friend was gay, and they spent a lot of time together, and he had always wanted to see Italy, so she said I'm going to be there for a month, so why don't you drop by and stay with me . . .

She was looking at him. "I hope he copes with Italian driving. He's never been here before."

"It's different."

She was still looking at him. "Are you all right?" she asked.

He was quick to reassure her. "Perfectly. I was just thinking about . . ." He waved a hand carelessly. "About artichoke soup."

"I like the sound of it," she said.

"Your friend," he blurted out. "What does he do?"

"Finance," she said. "He manages funds. He works in Boston. It's not ideal."

"Working in Boston?"

She smiled. "No, it's not the work—it's the fact that he has to live there and I'm a bit out of the city. Near a place called Concord—you may have heard of it. It's very important historically."

He had not. "We have different histories," he said. It was now quite clear. There was no other interpretation.

"The college I work at is not far from Concord. I have an apartment there. It's in the basement of a retired couple. It's great—they're very quiet and it's rather nice having them upstairs. She's a keen baker and makes me cookies. I have to pretend to eat them, but I actually give them away because she makes so many I'd put on pounds and pounds. But I don't want to offend her."

"Of course not."

"So I give them to my students. They like them. Students will eat anything."

"And drink anything too."

"He—that is, Mr. Ellis upstairs—he makes model ships

that he puts in bottles. You see them in antique stores but I never thought anybody still actually made them."

He said, "What's your friend's name?"

"Andrew."

There was silence for a few moments. Then he asked, "Have you been together long?"

"Forever."

He tried to smile. "Ah! A long time." He paused. "You must be looking forward to seeing him. When does he arrive?"

"In a few days. He hasn't yet told me exactly when."

"So if you go to Siena before then, you'll take the bus?"

"I guess so."

She seemed reluctant to say more about Andrew. For his part, Paul was struggling with his disappointment, so for a few moments both looked down at the tablecloth with studied intensity. Paul's dismay was profound: the affair he had been hoping for was thwarted at the very outset. She was spoken for—it was as simple as that. And of course she would be; after all, she was an extremely attractive young woman, intelligent, vivacious, witty; of course there would be somebody—there always was in such cases.

He swallowed hard. He would be adult about this. "I'm pleased that you have somebody coming to share this place with you." As he spoke, he thought: *You have no idea that what I feel is exactly the opposite of what I'm saying.*

She looked up. "Well, thank you. It's always nicer to have somebody to enjoy a place with—to have the right company."

He thought: *Me, me, me!*

"And what about you?" she asked.

In his misery he did not hear what she said.

"And you?" she repeated.

"Me? Well, no . . . I mean, I'm just here. Just me."

The look she gave him was a searching one. Noticing it, he saw that she was wanting to ask things that she did not want to spell out. He would make it easy.

"I was with somebody," he said. "I was with somebody for the last four years. Now it's over."

He realised that he had not entirely answered her question. Somebody could be anybody—male or female.

"She went off with somebody else, you see."

Again there was not enough information. Somebody else could also be anybody. Women left men for men or for women, just as men left women for other women or for men.

"For a man," he added. "She left me for her personal trainer."

This elicited a reaction. Anna's eyes—her flecked-green eyes, he noticed again—widened at the disclosure. "Really? A personal trainer?"

"Yes. He was . . ." Paul struggled. He did not want to appear bitter; those who are left, if bitter, can seem pathetic. He did not want that. But then again, why should he not tell her how he felt? Even if she was not going to be a lover, she could at least be a friend to whom he could speak openly. Who else did he have to speak to about such things while he was here? Onesto? Tonio? Neither of these seemed likely confidants.

"He was pretty awful," said Paul. "It's not that personal trainers, in themselves, are awful—they aren't . . ."

She interrupted him. "But a lot of them are. They're so energetic and keen. They run on the spot when they talk to you. They make you feel guilty. They inflict pain . . ." She smiled. "I'm exaggerating, of course, but I would never go off with a personal trainer. Never."

Her smile lifted his mood. "No, I'm sure you wouldn't.

There are those who would run off with a personal trainer . . . And one would *run*, wouldn't one, when going off with a personal trainer? One wouldn't walk."

She laughed. "They must be so exhausting. And going out for dinner with your personal trainer, you'd have to be so careful not to choose anything calorific. It would be salads every time."

He entered into the spirit of it. He became reckless. "And think of the physical side of the relationship. It would be so tiring . . ." He stopped himself. He had not meant to say it; he had meant to do no more than think it.

And now he could see that he had embarrassed her, as she glanced away.

"I'm sorry," he said. "That slipped out."

He felt bathed by her smile. It was like a soft light. "You don't have to say you're sorry. I was thinking the same thing myself."

"I think we should change the subject," he said. He felt better now; she would be just a friend; he would satisfy himself with that. And you can't go falling for every woman you meet on your bulldozer, he said to himself. He smiled at the thought.

"I'm going to Siena tomorrow," she said. "I'm taking the early bus."

They talked about Siena. Had she ever seen the Palio, the horse race round the main piazza that engaged passions for months and was over in a few hectic seconds? She had seen it on film, she said; she was not particularly interested in horse-racing.

"But it's not about horses," Paul said. "It's about local rivalries. It's the same thing here in Montalcino. They have an archery competition. And that's not really about archery.

Each quarter has its bowmen who practise like nobody's business for months and months. They provide an outlet for how people feel about their *quartiere*. That's what it's really about."

She looked thoughtful. "You could say that about a lot of sports, couldn't you? The actual game is about the place you live in, the people you're loyal to, and so on. It's not about throwing or kicking a ball or doing whatever it is you do to a ball."

The waiter came back with their first course—*Pappa al Pomodoro*—a tomato dish reeking of garlic, served with stale bread.

"The bread's meant to be like this," said Paul. "Fresh bread would be all wrong."

He had ordered a coastal white wine to accompany this course, and it was now served. He raised his glass to her, and she responded. As he sipped at the wine, he looked down into the straw-coloured liquid and thought: *She likes me. The way she's looking at me proves she likes me.* And then he allowed himself the thought: *What if she decided that she prefers me to this Andrew of hers? What if . . .* He stopped himself. There was no point in even beginning to think that. The fact that Andrew was coming all the way from Boston just to spend a week with her in Italy made it clear that he—and she, of course—was committed.

The conversation moved on to her artists. One of them, she said, had come from a village near Montalcino and had studied in Florence with Ghirlandaio. "The father, that is— Domenico Ghirlandaio. He had a son, Ridolfo, who was also a painter. Domenico did that famous picture in the Louvre— you may know it—of the man with the bulbous nose looking down on his grandson, who's looking up at him."

Paul knew it. *"An Old Man and His Grandson,"* he said.

"Yes. Anyway, he studied with him and then came back to Siena. He had a patron there, and he did a series of paintings for him. They're not considered particularly good, but I like them. I've written something about them."

Paul watched her as she spoke. You can always tell when people love their subject, he thought; their faces light up when they talk about it. And that was happening now. Mind you, he said to himself, her face did not light up when she talked about Andrew. Perhaps she was not looking forward to his visit as much as one might expect.

He was considering that possibility when she suddenly asked him, "Have you found somebody else?"

He had started his answer when she cut him off.

"Because if you haven't, have you been online? That's how people do it these days."

He shook his head. "I don't know."

She was solicitous. "You mustn't allow yourself to mope."

"I won't."

He felt a trickle of liquid tomato run down his chin, and dabbed at it with his table napkin. "Oh, well," he said.

"Yes," she said. "It's hard."

"Life?"

"Yes, life, but love in particular—that's the hard bit."

She picked up a piece of the stale bread and dipped it in the tomato stew. "Most people get through it somehow, don't they?"

They made their way through the courses. The conversation was light without being superficial. She told him about her parents, who had moved to Florida. He told her about how he had started writing books on food. And then, towards the end, they came to the *pecorino nero* and its trickle of honey.

"Even the honey has its complexities," said Paul. "They have a honey festival here each year."

"In Montalcino?"

"Honey producers from all over Italy come and sell their honey. If you want acacia honey, you can get it. If you want rose-scented honey, you can get that too. It's a whole world of its own."

She licked the honey off her fingers. "That cheese was fantastic," she said.

"I'll get hold of some for you."

"You mustn't bother." She smiled. "You're spoiling me. You've already rescued me from the roadside. You've arranged this dinner. And now you're going to go and find some black-fleeced sheep . . ."

He found that he wanted to do it for her; she was going to be no more than a friend, but he wanted to please her.

She suddenly seemed to remember something. "Your bulldozer," she said.

"Yes, my bulldozer."

"Where have you parked it?"

He was surprised by the question. "The usual place. Where I put it when I brought you back here."

She frowned. "But it wasn't there this afternoon. I went for a walk. I was down there and I looked for it."

"But it must be. You must have been at another car park."

She was adamant. "No, I was definitely in the right place."

He drew in his breath, and then exhaled slowly. "Are you absolutely sure?"

"Yes."

He let out a sigh. "Then it's been stolen."

"But who would steal a bulldozer?"

He shrugged. "I have no idea. I suppose I'll have to go and take a look."

"Right now?"

The evening, he thought, was going to end on a low note. "Would you mind? You see, I'll have to go to the police and report it. It's a rented bulldozer, and I'll need to get in touch with the people in Pisa."

She was apologetic. "I'm sorry to bring it up. It's just that . . ."

Paul had second thoughts. "I suppose we could do dessert. It's not going to make any difference." He had also suddenly realised that the bulldozer had probably been towed away for illegal parking. That was far more likely—and far less complicated. But he still wanted to see for himself—and perhaps there was a notice left where he had parked it: *This vehicle has been towed away by the authorities for illegal parking.*

"No. You can't sit there wondering what's happened. We should go."

He signalled to the waiter. "Change of plan," he said. "Sorry. No dessert."

The waiter looked at him reproachfully, but then, glancing at Anna, reached his conclusion. It was not unheard of for people to fall out at the table and for parties to break up before the end of the meal. People were unpredictable, he thought; that's one thing you learned as a waiter. He inclined his head, and went off to fetch the bill.

A Very Famous Pincher of Women

In the Fiaschetteria the next morning Onesto listened intently, his copy of *La Nazione* set aside, as Paul related the events of the previous evening.

"Gone?" he said. "Not there?"

"So my friend said. She was absolutely certain."

"And yet . . . and yet it was there? Where you had left it?"

"Exactly where I had left it. In its place. I saw it with my own eyes when we left the restaurant and looked down onto the car park. There's a streetlight down there—right next to where the bulldozer's parked—and so I couldn't have been mistaken."

Onesto raised an eyebrow. "And she saw it too? This lady saw it too?"

"Yes. We both did."

Onesto started to smile. "She must have been imagining things. Women can be funny about bulldozers . . ."

"She accepted that it was there. She agreed that it was definitely there when we looked, but that didn't change her mind about its absence before. She said that when she was down there in the afternoon it wasn't there. She looked for it, but it was gone."

Onesto sat back in his chair and stared out of the door. In the piazza, two young boys were taunting a small dog tied by its leash to a railing. The dog was frantically looking round for its owner while at the same time defending itself from the boys' prodding.

"Those two," muttered Onesto, pointing. "You see them? The older one is called Carlo and that's his cousin, Alfredo. We never went in for beating children in quite the same way as they did in England, but if we had, then those two would have been top of my list."

Paul followed his gaze. "You teach them?" he asked.

"I try to. But they come from very ignorant homes and it's difficult. The older one is very greedy and all he ever thinks about is eating. The younger one likes to look up the girls' skirts. I'm very worried about him." He sighed. "But then you look at his father, and you realise where it comes from. He was a very famous pincher of women before it started to be frowned upon in Italy. He used to travel down to Buonconvento on the bus just in order to pinch women as they walked past him to get to their seat. Then he'd come back on the same bus, and do exactly the same thing. It was his hobby." He shook his head. "Fortunately, Italy has changed since those days, at least up here. Women can still experience some of this nonsense down in the south."

There was a sudden shout from the piazza. The dog, prodded once too often by the older boy, had succeeded in nipping him on the ankle. The boy was about to retaliate with a kick when the dog's owner returned and directed loud invective at his pet's tormentors.

"Good," said Onesto. "That lady is the chemist's cousin. She has three sons of her own, and she knows how to deal with boys." He turned to face Paul again. "I think this friend of yours, this lady . . ."

"Anna."

"This Anna may have been right after all. I think your bull-dozer was used by somebody. It happens. People help them-selves round here. They take the view that if something isn't being used, then there's no harm in borrowing it for a while. I think that may have happened to your bulldozer." He paused. "And I assume it's all right—nothing damaged?"

Paul explained that he had gone down to check up that all was well, and there was no sign of any damage. "But why would somebody borrow a bulldozer?"

Onesto shrugged. "To dig a ditch, perhaps? People are always digging ditches." He smiled. "I always say, *We have enough ditches,* but people say, *Oh no, we need more.* You know how it is. There are people who simply want more ditches."

Paul finished his coffee. "I remain puzzled," he said.

Onesto had more to say. "Yes, it is a bit puzzling. Of course, it's always possible . . ." He broke off and seemed to play with an idea. "Perhaps."

"Perhaps what?"

"Perhaps some task of destruction. You see, bulldozers are good for knocking things down. Perhaps somebody wants to knock something down—there are plenty of people who would like to see some things knocked down. I have my own list. Perhaps that's what your bulldozer has been used for."

"But you can't go about knocking things down."

Onesto made a dismissive sound. "Pah! You can do any-thing in this country. Rome is so weak. They're busy fighting with one another down there while all over the place there are people using European Union money to build things we don't need, and then other people come along and knock them down. This happens all the time."

Paul looked at his watch. "I have to get to work."

Onesto reached for his paper. "And I must return to this."

He pointed to a headline, and shook his head sadly. "I could have told them this would happen. But did they ask me? They did not."

"They never do," said Paul. "They never ask us."

This anodyne remark seemed to resonate with Onesto. "You'd think they'd learn."

Paul paid for his coffee and said goodbye to Onesto. Then he turned to leave the Fiaschetteria and walked straight into Becky, who was standing outside, admiring the café's elaborate fin de siècle sign.

She opened her arms. "Darling," she said, "Paulie . . ."

He grimaced. He hated being called Paulie.

She had taken a step forward, ready to embrace him, but stopped herself. "You *are* pleased to see me? Please tell me you're pleased to see me."

He struggled to control himself. "Did you get my message?"

She made a dismissive gesture. "Oh that . . . I saw something, but I'd already arrived in Rome. I could hardly go back. All I want to do is talk to you."

He cast about him in desperation. He could hardly run away, and now he found that he did not want to. He looked at her and realised that it was not as easy to forget as he had imagined. He had wanted to forget her, but here she was, and for a moment he saw himself with her, in her embrace, and he remembered how it was.

He closed his eyes.

She reached out to touch his arm; she was aware of her power over him. "Aren't you going to buy me a cup of coffee? Surely that?"

There were seats free at one of the outside tables. He gestured towards them, almost helplessly.

"We've got so much to talk about," she said as they sat down.

"Becky . . ."

She put a finger to her lips. "Not now, though. All I want to say now is one word. Sorry." She paused. She was looking at him with unrelenting intensity. "There, I've said it, and I'll say it again: Sorry." There was a further pause, and then, "See?"

Paul sighed. "You don't have to say sorry."

He had intended to go on, but Becky immediately reached forward and gripped his arm again. "Of course I do," she said. "The separation was my idea."

It was the first time he had heard her use the term. Separation could be temporary; theirs was a break-up.

"I don't think I'd describe it that way . . ."

Again she interrupted him. "But that's what it was. You must have known that. Lots of couples separate. In fact . . ." She squeezed his arm, as if to emphasise her point. "In fact, I've read that there are relationship counsellors who *advise* a trial separation every so often—just to make sure that people know what they really want. Most of them get back together." Once more there was a pause before she continued, "Not that I'm planning that."

She smiled, as if explaining something to one who was a bit slow in such matters. "But we are friends again, aren't we? I've said sorry. You've said sorry. And now we find ourselves in this gorgeous place." She looked around her appreciatively. "I was going to stay only one night, but I think I'll extend it. Perhaps I'll stay three or four days . . ."

He gasped, and she heard. She looked at him with concern. "Don't worry. I've taken a room at a hotel. I'll make my own arrangements."

His voice sounded weak. "Which hotel?"

"The Fiore. Just down there." She pointed to the lane off the piazza. "It's very romantic. Do you know it?"

He nodded miserably. "I'm staying there."

This brought a laugh. "Well, that's a coincidence."

"Yes. But, Becky, I really think the whole thing . . . Why did you think you had to come all the way to Italy just to say sorry?"

She fixed him with a piercing stare. "Because I've felt guilty. I've felt so bad about it that I thought the only way I could deal with it was to come and speak to you. You know how it is when you've really hurt somebody—you feel that the only way of getting back to normal is facing them—speaking to them directly."

"You didn't have to . . ."

She raised a finger. "Ssh! Let's just sit here and think positive thoughts."

Paul looked up at the sky. As he did so, he heard the familiar ping with which his mobile heralded the arrival of a text message.

"Popular man," said Becky. "But then you always were, weren't you?"

Paul fished the phone out of his pocket. Shielding the screen from the sunlight, he read the message. It was from Gloria. *Heard of what's going on. Are you okay? I'm on my way. Will get in touch to let you know when arriving. Good old British Airways to Pisa. Will get train if they still exist. G.*

Paul realised that Becky was staring at him. "Good news?" she asked. "Major television series?"

"No. Nothing."

She persisted, and he remembered how she had always read his e-mails without asking his permission. Becky was nosy. "A friend?" she asked.

"My editor."

Becky smiled. "Oh, her—what's-her-face?"

"Gloria," said Paul sharply.

"Sorry! I forgot. She's the boss."

He felt that he had to defend her. "She's not the boss—and she never tries to be the boss. She's the most helpful, considerate, loyal . . ." He dwelt on the word *loyal,* but Becky showed no reaction. "The most *loyal* editor you could ever want."

"Oh, a saint," said Becky. "Of course." And then, as if realising that she had irritated Paul, she drew back. "No, you're right. Gloria's fab."

Paul was thinking. A minor disaster had become a major one. Gloria and Becky had never got on well, and even though they had never openly argued or fought, Becky's simmering dislike for the editor had always been apparent just below the surface.

"So what did she say?" asked Becky.

"Nothing," answered Paul.

"Why would she text if she had nothing to say?"

Paul slipped the phone back into his pocket. "It's my business," he said.

Becky bit her lip. "I wasn't prying."

Paul looked at her. "Becky, I think we need to get one thing clear. I know you've come a long way . . ."

"Actually, the flight to Rome isn't long at all. I had a good book to read. By that woman—I forget what she's called—the one with the odd name—I find it really difficult to remember people who aren't called something simple, you know how it is . . ."

He ignored this. "And that thing, Becky, is this: it's *over.* Over." He sighed. "I'm really sorry, and I don't want to be unkind, but it really is over. O . . . V . . . E . . . R. You, me—over."

She looked down at the tablecloth. "Okay, you've said it, and I've got the message. You didn't think I wanted to start again, did you?"

He was unsure. There was something about the situation that made him feel uneasy. Had she really come just to apologise, or was she secretly hoping that they might pick up where they had left off? "Have you really got the message? Have you really got it?"

"Of course I have. I'm not one to press myself on anybody. I can pick up the vibe."

"Good."

"But all I'd say is this: give our friendship a chance. Give it a chance over the next few days. Let's see what happens."

He drew in his breath. It would require all his patience— he could see that—but perhaps he owed it to her. They had been together for four years, and the least he could do was to be civil to her while she was here. She would go and that would be that, but in the meantime there was no need for him to be unkind.

"I don't think there's much chance of our being close friends," he said.

She immediately seized on this. "Not *much* chance, but still *some* chance. That's all I ask for, Paul—that's all."

He looked away. "What about that guy?"

"What guy? You mean Tommy?"

He nodded. "Yes, your personal trainer."

"It's still fine between him and me. But Tommy has some issues."

He waited for her to continue, but she was silent.

"What sort of issues?"

"Major issues."

He raised an eyebrow. "Well, why did you go off with him? What did you see in him?"

"I didn't know about his issues. Come on, Paul, when you meet somebody in the gym, you can't tell what his issues are. How can you? It's when you get . . . when you get out there that issues come up."

"Well then, maybe you should be more careful about people you meet in the gym. Maybe they're there to work out their issues."

"You don't have to rub it in, Paul. Subject closed, okay? Tommy and I are still an item. You don't have to worry about that."

$\mathcal{H}$e escorted her back to the Fiore before excusing himself for work.

"I have to get on with things," he said. "I came here to finish my book."

She said that she understood. "What time shall we meet for dinner?"

He did not answer immediately. He was struck by her presumption: How did she know that he did not have existing arrangements? But then he told himself it would be churlish to refuse to have a meal with her—at least on the first day of her trip. He replied that he would meet her downstairs in the Fiore at seven and he would take her somewhere he thought would appeal to her.

"Just like the old days," she said.

He was non-committal as he said goodbye. Then he made his way to his room and began to unlock his door. He heard a noise behind him—a creak in the floorboards. He turned round, half expecting to see her, but the corridor was empty.

He let himself into his room and went to his desk. Now he had time to consider what he would do about Gloria—not that he thought he could do very much. It seemed to him that there was no point in his trying to discourage visitors—they came anyway. Who would be next? His dentist? His hairdresser?

Paul sat down and stared at the papers before him. There was a draft chapter on the desk, so heavily annotated now that he would have to type it out afresh. That would be a dull repetitive task that would at least allow him to think out strategies for dealing with the Becky problem, or the Becky–Gloria problem—a name every bit as ominous and fraught with difficulties as the Schleswig–Holstein Question.

He was distracted by a sound outside his door. Again it was the creaking of a floorboard. He rose to his feet and crossed the room quietly. Standing near the door, he listened carefully. At first he heard nothing, but then he made out what seemed to him to be the sound of somebody breathing; it was slightly laboured, as is the breathing of one who has walked upstairs or has become excited. He strained to hear more, but the breathing only became fainter. A floorboard creaked; whoever it was—and he imagined that it must be Becky—was retreating down the corridor.

He opened the door as quietly as he could and peered outside. There was nobody there, and the silence was complete. Somewhere off down the hill, a bell began to toll—an unfamiliar bell, the sound being carried up the slopes on the breeze. He closed his door and returned to his desk. *Mushrooms in Tuscan cuisine.* The heading stared out at him, and below it the sentence, *You never know what you'll stumble upon in Tuscany, particularly in a Tuscan wood at the right time of year.* No, you did not. Mushrooms—of course—but other surprises too; and not just in a Tuscan wood—in a Tuscan café, in a Tuscan corridor too.

It occurred to him that there was a way out of his difficulties. He could pack his bags, carry them down to the car park, and set off on his bulldozer. He could go somewhere else—to a place where nobody, not even Gloria, would be able to find him—to Montepulciano, perhaps, or even to a small village he had visited some years earlier, where nobody would know him, to San Casciano dei Bagni, in the southernmost reaches of Tuscany. He would be able to finish the book there, undisturbed, and was there any rule to prevent one from avoiding uninvited guests?

Of course there was not—or at least not a specific rule. But he was not one to run away, and there was always simple decency, the principles of which certainly dictated that you owed something to somebody who had given you four years of her life. The least you could do was allow her four days, even if you were adamant that nothing was to be rekindled in that time.

Paul sighed and began to write, "Porcini mushrooms are not a single variety of mushroom, but a whole range of related fungi. *Porcini* means *piglets* and these mushrooms indeed have a very palatable meaty taste to them . . ."

He wrote for half an hour, the words coming with ease and conviction. One could feel intensely about mushrooms, he found himself thinking: such *independent* things, so *undemanding,* so rewarding when added to virtually any dish. And it was while he was in mid-flow, singing the praises of Italian mushroom culture, that he heard the ping of a text arriving. This time he hardly dared look, but when he plucked up his courage and did so his heart sank. *Just left Pisa!* wrote Gloria.

Will stop on the way for lunch. See you at the Fiore. Dinner tonight in lovely little family trattoria? Can't wait! G.

He closed his eyes and imagined himself on the bulldozer, the great machine lumbering beneath him, the wind in his hair, and heading south for the Mezzogiorno, along routes that have always meant freedom for those bent on escape from the north and all it stood for.

II

Love Is a Soufflé

$\mathcal{H}$e did not dare go out for lunch, but made do with some biscuits and a half-depleted packet of fig rolls he had tucked away in a drawer. Montalcino was too small a place to be able to walk the streets with any assurance that one would not meet somebody one was avoiding—a bad place, clearly, to end up with a former lover. At least he felt safe in his room, sequestered with his work table and its pile of papers, while Becky, he presumed, explored the village.

He felt bad about her. He did not dislike her, as some people did their former lovers; there was a lot about her that he enjoyed and admired. Nor did he entirely blame her for running off with the personal trainer; he had been preoccupied with his work and had probably not given her enough of his time. But even if that had not happened, he thought it likely that they would have drifted apart: the magic, the chemistry, the spark—those ingredients that had provided the seasoning for their relationship—had begun to fade well before they split up, and he thought that none of that could now be recovered. Love was a soufflé that could only too easily collapse and could rarely be revived. And he had no such desire to attempt that now, even if her very presence had kindled in him a nostalgia for the human intimacy that his life now lacked. Yes, he thought, I can imagine myself waking up with her, opening the shutters of this room and looking out over the valley below; bringing her a cup of tea in bed; staring up at the ceiling with her while planning the day ahead. Yes, he thought, I *am* lonely here, and I would not be lonely with her. Yet she had no right to come barging in on him. It showed a trait in her character that he had always been aware of, but that had not been quite so clearly displayed as it now was— a tactlessness, a pushiness that verged on the boorish. Becky was insensitive to the feelings of others; he had seen it in her before but had not thought much about it—not easy now that he was at the receiving end of it. What sensitive person would have taken it upon herself to intrude on another's retreat—and she must have known that the reason he had come to Italy was to finish off his book. She simply had not thought the whole thing through; it was the sort of thing an impulsive eighteen-year-old might do—an impulsive, and selfish, eighteen-year-old.

He thought of Anna, and he realised that he could never be happy with Becky again knowing, as he now did, that there were people like Anna: tactful, intelligent people, who could excite him intellectually in a way in which poor Becky never could. Not that there is any future with Anna, he thought ruefully. Unless . . . No, he made a conscious effort to put the thought out of his mind. He would arrive—her man from Boston—and she would have time only for him; he would see the two of them in the Fiaschetteria, perhaps, or in one of the restaurants, lost in each other, while he, an observer of the pleasure of others, would look on, a newspaper or book on the table beside him in case he got too bored with his own company, which he would.

And he—the boyfriend—would say to her, "Who *is* that at the table over there? That rather sad person, all by himself?"

And she would say, "Oh, he's just somebody who writes stuff about food and wine and who drives a bulldozer."

To which he would respond, "Poor guy" or "Sad, isn't it?" or something of that sort, and their conversation would move on and no more attention would be paid to him.

In spite of such musings he surprised himself how much work he managed to get done, and by early afternoon he had finished the chapter that he had thought would take him the entire day. He had said everything he intended to say about porcini mushrooms and indeed about mushrooms of every sort. He had written several paragraphs on the pleasures of the hunt for rare varieties and on the sort of trees under which the various mushrooms liked to grow. He had almost a page on the transporting and drying of wild mushrooms— on the need to use a basket rather than a plastic container, as plastic was apt to damage the delicate flesh of the mushroom. He had half a page on the best way to produce *funghi trifolati* in the classic Italian manner and a small section on the art of reviving dried mushrooms. And with that, as he closed the lid of his laptop on the world of mushrooms, he decided what to do about that evening. He had put off making a decision, but now he had run out of time. He had imagined that Gloria would arrive around three, and that he would by then have some idea of what he was going to do. It was now half past two.

With new decisiveness he began to write a note to Becky. *Changed plans, I'm afraid,* he began. *I can't do dinner tonight— sorry about that. But let's do lunch tomorrow—I promise! I'll see you around ten in the morning and we can go off to a restaurant I know down the Grosseto road. Have you ever ridden on a bulldozer? (That's a serious question, by the way.) All will be revealed tomorrow. Paul.*

He read what he had written. There were no lies: he had

simply said that he could not do dinner. Disinclination to do something was as good a reason as any for saying that one could not do it . . . He put down the note. He could not send a note like that. So he changed "I can't do dinner" to "I don't feel up to dinner tonight." That was absolutely truthful. He did not feel up to it. But even then there was something shameful about the note; why could he not tell Becky this to her face? Surely that was the honourable thing to do, and yet if he tried to speak to her about this she would not take no for an answer. She would try to make him change his mind and she had always been particularly good at that. He looked at the note again and made another change. "I don't feel up to dinner tonight" became "I don't feel up to dinner with you tonight." That was even more strictly true: he did not feel disinclined to have dinner; it was just that he did not want to have it with her.

He groaned. He felt appalled at himself, but what alternative did he have? Was there any moral obligation to go out to dinner with somebody who was forcing herself on you? No, there was not. He would be strong. He would protect himself against an unwarranted intrusion on his privacy. Becky should not have come, and she had no right to browbeat him into anything. And yet, and yet . . .

He folded the note neatly and stood up. Then he wrote her name on the outside of an envelope: *Ms. Becky Rogers, Room* . . . He was not sure what to write, and so he crossed out *Room* and wrote, *In residence.* There was something rather grand about that; that was how great hotels described their guests: they were in residence. Somehow it seemed out of place in the Fiore, but he left it as it was, went downstairs and handed the note to Ella, whom he found poring over a register in reception.

She examined the note. "Room Four," she said. "I shall hand it to your fiancée. She is out for a walk at the moment."

Paul drew in his breath. "My fiancée?"

"That is what she said to me," said Ella. She hesitated. "You're not engaged?"

Paul shook his head.

"I see," said Ella. She was searching Paul's face for some clue to the mystery. "Perhaps she thinks you're engaged. Do you think that possible?"

"Possible," said Paul. "But I assure you, we're not."

Ella looked embarrassed. "She said that she would only be needing Room Four for one night. Now she wants to have it for four, but she can't, and I can't give her another one. Everything's booked up. There's somebody coming tomorrow. The room will be needed."

For a moment Paul was uncertain what to say. Ella was looking at him strangely—not so much with an air of disapproval as of puzzlement.

He wiped his forehead without thinking, but a great deal can be said with the hands in Italy, and the message this conveyed was the right one.

Ella's tone became sympathetic. "I can see that you're in some difficulty," she said. "This lady . . . I think she's pursuing you."

Paul nodded gratefully. "I don't think so. I think she's a bit confused." He paused before continuing. "We used to be together and then . . ."

He was not sure whether he should say anything further. He did not wish to burden Ella with his emotional entanglements, and yet he felt that here was an understanding ear—and a useful ally.

"May I tell you about it?" he asked.

He need not have been concerned; she was ready to hear what he had to say. And when his explanation drew to a close, he could tell from her expression that she had understood.

"It's not always the man," she mused. "It's often the woman. I've seen that so many times."

"Oh yes?"

"Yes. In my profession, you know, one sees all of human nature." She raised a finger to emphasise the point. "All. There are no secrets that an innkeeper does not know; there is no human behaviour—none—that would surprise us."

Paul's eyes widened. For a brief moment he imagined the discoveries made in rooms after people had vacated them, the conversations overheard, the demands made, the things left behind . . .

"And when it comes to bad behaviour," Ella continued, "it's equally split—in my view. Fifty-fifty between men and women."

"As it should be," said Paul.

"You see," Ella continued, "there are many women who assume that it is always the man who acts badly. If there is any problem between a man and a woman, they think, *Ah yes, this will be another example of bad behaviour by men.* But it's not that simple. Yes, there are men who behave badly, who will get rid of a woman when somebody better turns up, who throw women aside without so much as . . ."

Not me, thought Paul. *I didn't.*

". . . without so much as a thought for the feelings of the poor woman. And then you get women who do exactly the same thing to men. Or who make the life of the man unbearable with jealousy and reproach. Or who come between him and the things that any man likes to do. Or who work out all their anger on him. Oh yes, there are many women who behave every bit as badly as men do."

"I'm sure there are," said Paul. "Becky—this lady—she's not like that. She did go off with somebody—as I told you—but she's not what we would call a shrew."

Ella was interested in the term. "A shrew? One of those little creatures like a field-mouse?"

"Yes. Perhaps it's unfair to shrews, but people call very forceful women shrews. Or used to."

"But you just did."

"No, I didn't really mean it. I meant . . . what other people would call a shrew." He thought of Shakespeare. "Shakespeare for example. One of his plays is all about that, and the shrew in that is a difficult woman. *Commedia dell'arte*. Same thing."

"So this lady—this Signora Becky—is not a mouse?"

"Shrew. No. She's not."

"But she is still somebody you would rather avoid?"

Paul took a deep breath. "It's not a question of avoiding her. As I said, I don't want to be unkind to her. I just want to get on with my life."

This brought vigorous agreement from Ella. "Which is all that most of us want to do. We want to get on with our lives—without interference from Rome, or from Brussels." She paused, as if to mull over an idea. "I can make arrangements, I think."

Paul looked at her with interest. "For Becky?"

"Yes. There is a place down the road, the Pensione Garibaldi. They take overflow from us from time to time, and the other way round. They've never failed to find a room for somebody when I've asked them. We're on very good terms."

Paul brightened. "So they'll be able to take Becky?"

Ella said that she thought they would.

"Then that solves that."

Ella smiled. "I'm sorry that you are having all this difficulty, Paolo. You come here for peace and quiet, on your bulldozer, and you find yourself running away from a woman. It's very unfortunate."

Paul wondered how she knew about the bulldozer, but did not ask. It was obvious to him now that Montalcino was not a place in which secrets of any sort would survive for long. He looked at his watch: Gloria could arrive at any time.

"There's one further thing, Ella. I'm expecting a colleague this afternoon. I am going to be in my room."

Ella was briskly efficient. "I shall refer him to you immediately."

"Her. It's a lady."

Paul could tell what she was thinking. "It's not what you imagine," he said. "This lady is my editor."

"Your *editor*?" The word was uttered in inverted commas.

"I assure you she is," said Paul. "She's here because she heard that the other lady had followed me."

Ella hesitated, and Paul realised that her quandary now was that of deciding in which of the fifty per cents to place him. But then she broke into a smile and he knew that he was believed.

"You know, we do not expect the English to have such interesting lives. We expect it of the Spanish and the French, perhaps, but not the English."

"Scottish."

"Yes, Scottish. It seems very strange." She closed her register. "But don't worry. I shall speak to nobody about this. The important thing is that you should be able to get on with your work."

He thanked her and went back upstairs to his room, passing Room Four on the way, treading softly as he made his way along the corridor in case Becky might have returned. *I don't have to do any of this,* he thought. *I shouldn't have to creep around like a criminal.* And then he thought of Occhidilupo. He pictured him skulking around the woods, his dark eyes watchful and wary. What if Occhidilupo were to surface in the Fiore, or even in the Fiaschetteria, brooding over a cup of coffee, scanning *La Nazione* for the latest reports of sightings of himself? Nothing would surprise him in Italy—even that. *Commedia dell'arte,* he thought.

Paul had dozed off when Ella knocked on his door. "Your colleague," she said, placing heavy emphasis on the word, "is downstairs. Shall I bring her up?"

He decided to meet her downstairs and went down to find Gloria sitting in the reception hall's single chair, a small valise by her side. She sprang to her feet and rushed towards him. Ella, glancing briefly at Paul, went off to busy herself with some task in her office.

The first thing that Gloria said was, "You're not cross with me, are you?"

"Cross?"

"For coming here?"

He drew back from her embrace. "Not really." He paused. "You heard about . . ." Involuntarily he glanced upstairs, and Gloria intercepted his look.

"Is she there?"

He shook his head. "Not at the moment, but I'd prefer for us to go somewhere else. There's a place called the Fiaschetteria—you'll like it."

Gloria looked down at her luggage. "May I leave my bag?"

"Of course," said Paul. "I can put it in my room."

He reached for the bag and began to make for the stairs. She followed him.

"Do you mind if I come and see?" she asked. "I've been trying to imagine the place you're working in."

He led her along the corridor. "That's her room," he whispered, as they passed Room Four.

Gloria gave the doorway a disapproving glance. "Shameless!" she whispered back, smiling conspiratorially. "She's a stalker, that's what she is."

"No," said Paul. "She isn't. And actually, I feel a bit sorry for her."

"Because she's stuck with Mr. Universe? Is that why?"

"No, not that." He struggled to think of how he could explain. "Because she's . . . well, lonely, I suppose."

"You can bring loneliness on yourself," said Gloria. "And she's terribly mixed up."

"Aren't we all?" said Paul. "In a way?"

They had reached Paul's door, and he admitted them to the room. Gloria looked around, and then crossed to the open window. "Look at that," she exclaimed. "That could be a Renaissance painting. Oh, beautiful, beautiful country!" She turned to Paul. "Why didn't we have the good luck to be born Italian, Paul? Is it something we did in a previous life? Something that led to bad karma?"

"I think a lot of people would like to be something else," said Paul. "Even Italians."

She pointed out of the window. "That sky . . . And the cypress trees. And the birds flying *below* us, Paul—*below* us."

He followed her gaze out of the window. Because the land

fell away so steeply, and because the Fiore—and the village—were on a spine of high ground, there were birds down below them, darting swallows in pursuit of insects. In the distance, rising from the floor of the Val d'Orcia, was a column of white smoke, as thin from this distance as the smoke of a snuffed-out candle. For a few moments he found himself reflecting on what it would be like to have a less complicated life; what it would be like to be the farmer burning brushwood, not caring about what was happening in the wider world, and not having to juggle social commitments and deadlines, not having to cope with former lovers with a vague agenda of forgiveness and friendship—or possibly more, as the lonely hearts columns put it—and protective editors.

Gloria looked around the room again. She noticed the twin beds, one of which Paul had occupied, the other being undisturbed.

She smiled at him. "An awkward question—but I feel I know you well enough."

"Yes?" He was hesitant.

"I haven't actually got anywhere to stay tonight. Tomorrow, yes, I've got a room here, but not tonight." She glanced at the spare bed. "Do you think I could? Just as a friend, of course. Chinese walls."

He drew in his breath. It had not occurred to him that she was the person who had telephoned to book the room to be vacated by Becky. "Isn't there anywhere else . . ." He stopped himself. Gloria had come all this way because she thought he needed help; he could not turn her down. "No," he continued. "I mean, yes. Yes, you can stay here."

"I shall behave myself impeccably," said Gloria. "I don't snore or talk in my sleep."

She moved across to the spare bed and drew it further

away from the other bed. "There," she said. "Plenty of blue sea between us."

Paul pointed towards his work table. "You see what a good boy I'm being. I'm keeping strictly to my timetable."

Gloria laughed. "I wouldn't have imagined otherwise. But I was worried that . . . that your ex was going to derail everything."

Ex? He had never thought of Becky as his ex.

"That's a strange term," he said. "I'm not sure if it suits her."

"Well, that's what she is—she's an ex. The problem is, though, that sometimes an ex can be difficult."

"I'm all right," said Paul. "I appreciate your concern, but I think everything's going to be all right."

Gloria was staring at him intently. "Are you sure?"

"Yes, more or less."

Gloria reached out to touch him lightly on the arm. "You have to be careful, Paul. She probably doesn't know what she wants. But you don't really owe her anything. I know you, Paul—you're so kind and considerate that you'll probably let yourself be dragooned back into a relationship—if that's what she's really after. And she may be, for all we know. But that's not what you want, is it?"

He looked down at the floor. "Oh, Gloria, I don't know— I really don't. There's a bit of me that says yes, why not? If she were to ask me to come back."

She shook her head vigorously. "No, Paul, no. Don't listen to that bit."

Paul moved over to the window. The column of smoke down in the valley had disappeared. "But there's something else—something I haven't told you."

Gloria frowned. "She's not pregnant, is she?"

"No, not to my knowledge."

Gloria's eyes widened. She had thought of something. Of course. Of course. "She could be, you know. Let's say that Mr. Universe . . ."

"He's called Tommy."

"Of course he's called Tommy—it's a very good name for a personal trainer. So Tommy gets her pregnant and then we don't see him for dust—not part of the plan. She looks around and thinks—somebody's going to have to provide for the child and so she decides . . ."

He interrupted her. "That's not a problem these days. She doesn't have to have the baby."

"No, that's true. But let's say that she wants it. The biological clock and so on."

"Well, she could just go ahead and have it. She wouldn't need me."

But Gloria thought she would. "Being a single mother isn't everybody's idea of bliss, Paul."

"I don't think she's pregnant. She was always very careful about that."

Gloria seemed unconvinced. "All right, we'll leave that to one side." She paused. "So what did you want to tell me?"

Paul moved away from the window to sit down on his bed. "I think I'm in love."

For a few moments she said nothing, the set of her mouth demonstrating her dismay. "With her? With Becky?"

He looked up in astonishment. "No, of course not."

"Who then?"

He told her of his meeting with Anna. "I can't get her out of my mind," he said. "I hardly know her, and yet . . . well, I'm smitten—that's all there is to it. I'm completely smitten."

She sat down next to him. "Just think about this very, very

carefully," she said. "You're on the rebound from Becky. It may not be the best time."

"And there's another thing. She already has somebody."

This was greeted with silence. Eventually Gloria spoke. "Well, that settles that, then. You're going to have to forget her. You don't have much choice, do you?"

"I know. But I can't—I just can't."

Gloria sighed. When she spoke, she sounded like a patient teacher, explaining to a child how the world is. "Listen, Paul—we all go through this at some stage in life. We fall for somebody we can't have. The lesson you learn from it is quite simple. You have to put the other person out of your mind. You have to accept it's not to be."

"I know that."

"Do you?"

"Yes, I do. But it hasn't stopped me feeling the way I feel." He paused, struggling to describe how he felt. "I feel raw. Do you know that feeling? As if I'm somehow exposed. Raw."

She took his hand. "Love hurts. That's what they say, isn't it? Love hurts."

"Yes, it does. It hurts a lot."

She stroked his hand gently. He found the gesture comforting.

"Do you want to come home?" she asked.

"No."

"Are you sure?"

He nodded. "Definitely. I'll be all right. I'll get over it."

Gloria gave his hand a squeeze. "We all do. We get over it. I've had to do that twice. I've . . ." But she stopped. It was as if she had said too much.

He realised that he knew nothing of Gloria's emotional

life. It seemed strange to him that she should even bother about such things: sensible, in-control Gloria, whose job it was to look after other people and not go off and get herself into emotional entanglements. He looked at her with new eyes. "You? Twice?"

She looked away. "You seem so surprised."

He was flustered. "I'm sorry. I don't think of you in that light, you see."

There was a forced briskness in her voice. "The first time," she said, "was when I was about sixteen. There was a boy at school who seemed to me to be just the most wonderful creature ever. He had dark hair and blue eyes—you know that combination—and I couldn't take my eyes off him. But he didn't so much as notice me. I tried everything, but it seemed as if I didn't exist. I think he didn't have much time for girls."

Paul sympathised. "I think most of us have had that experience."

"Yes. But it doesn't get any easier, does it?"

She let go of his hand; so simple to do, but so hard.

12

You Shouldn't Underestimate Hens

*I*t was only his third time at the restaurant, but they treated him like a regular. Word had got out that he was a famous food critic; he wrote for *The New York Times,* it was whispered by some; he was a Michelin inspector, others said; and yet others reported that he was writing a book that would declare Montalcino to be the culinary capital of Italy and that already a new hotel was being planned to deal with the expected influx of visitors. This hotel was to be built and run by the Swedes, the rumour went, but nobody was able to say why this should be so. In the midst of all this wild speculation, Paul was now given new and elaborate respect, particularly on his entry to the Stracotto, where the exchange of knowing glances indicated that even if it were to be true that he was a Michelin inspector, there was nothing here with which he could find fault.

Gloria sniffed at the air. "You wouldn't even have to eat anything," she said. "The cooking smells would be enough."

"That's the truffled lasagne," said Paul. "Some people find the smell of truffles a little bit overpowering."

"They're wrong," said Gloria firmly. "They're simply wrong."

It was a favourite expression of hers, and Paul, recognising it, smiled. There had been many occasions when he had heard her bringing some meandering or fruitless discussion to an end by saying, *You're simply wrong.* It was hard to argue with such a position, although he had occasionally retorted, *You're the one who's wrong,* but this had never worked.

It was a small restaurant, and they were the first to arrive that evening. As they sat over the aperitif produced for them by the owner, a second couple arrived, young Danes, followed, shortly afterwards, by an elderly man who had the look of a local and who entered into a long conversation through the door of the kitchen.

Gloria enquired what they were talking about.

"His hens," said Paul, his voice lowered. "He's telling her about his hens. They've developed some sort of staggering illness and they've been wandering round his yard like drunken sailors."

"Oh dear."

There came a torrent of advice from within the kitchen.

"And?" asked Gloria.

Paul listened. "She says that her aunt had that trouble, but they seemed to get better. She said she thought it was something they'd eaten. She says that hens have more delicate stomachs than people imagine. She also says that it could be psychological."

"I don't think so," said Gloria.

Paul smiled as he listened to what was being said at the kitchen door.

"He says that he doesn't believe that hens have psychological problems because their brains are too small. He says that hens haven't got the first clue about anything."

This drew a short reply from the kitchen.

"And she says that you shouldn't underestimate hens."

The waiter returned to take their order. He nodded appreciatively as Paul chose. "Precisely, *professore*," he said. "That is precisely what I would recommend."

"*Professore!*" whispered Gloria.

The waiter made his way back to the kitchen and Paul turned to Gloria, raising his glass in a toast. And it was at that point that Becky came in.

Paul froze.

Gloria, with her back to the door, had not noticed. "How did you find this place?" she asked Paul. "It's perfect . . ."

Her voice trailed off. Noticing Paul's gaze, she half-turned in her chair, and saw Becky. She had picked up her glass to touch it against Paul's; now she lowered it. She stared hard at the empty plate at the side of her place, as if studying the faded blue design.

Becky faltered, but the waiter had returned and pointed to a table. He drew a chair back for her, and she sat down. She looked up at the ceiling, at the walls; she did not look in Paul's direction.

"I'm going to have to say something," whispered Paul. "I'm sorry, but this place is too small. We can't sit here and pretend."

"Are you going to invite her over?" asked Gloria. "I don't mind if you do."

Paul looked agonised. "I can't."

"What else can you do? We can't sit here and whisper about somebody on the other side of the room."

Paul rose to his feet. As he did so, Becky looked up. She started to stand up too.

He stood before her. "Look," he said. "Gloria's turned up."

Becky had a table napkin in her hands. She was twisting it about her fingers. "So I see."

"Business," said Paul.

Becky stared at him. "You liar," she said.

"Why? She's my editor. You know that."

Becky's voice rose. "You didn't take long, did you? Get rid of me and then . . . her."

"I'm sorry. I don't think you know what you're talking about."

"Oh, I don't, do I? You can't do dinner tonight. You don't want to go out to dinner, do you? And I come in here and there you are with that woman."

He tried to defend himself. "It's not that simple."

The couple at the nearby table shifted uncomfortably in their seats.

Paul tried to calm her. "I don't think we should have a public row," said Paul.

"Oh you don't, do you?" Everyone was silent, and her voice resonated in the chambered ceiling. The man with the staggering hens looked on, his jaw dropping; the young couple stared fixedly at the menu.

And then Becky reached down to the table and took a fork. Lunging forward, she drove it into Paul's hand. He shouted out, and the fork dropped to the floor. Gloria pushed her chair back and leapt to Paul's defence. A glass toppled and fell, shattered on the floor.

Becky turned round and walked out of the door, every eye following her before going back to Paul, who was staring mutely at his hand. There was a small amount of blood; three punctures where the points of the fork had broken the skin.

The owner rushed to Paul's side. "*Professore,*" he said, reaching out to examine the injured hand. "Oh, *professore,* what a terrible thing to happen. She must be a madwoman."

"She was upset," said Paul.

"Upset?" shouted Gloria. "Upset!"

Paul was strangely calm. "Look, let's not make a fuss. It was an accident."

"An accident?" said Gloria. "I saw it, Paul. She stabbed you with a fork. I saw her."

Paul brought his hand to his mouth and sucked at the wound. "Nothing. It's nothing. A tiny drop of blood, that's all. And I think she was just trying to emphasise her point and it . . . well, it went wrong."

"I have something for this hand," said the owner. "I have a plaster."

He went back into the kitchen, past his wife, who was staring out from the kitchen doorway, her face a picture of astonishment and disbelief. Returning with a plaster, the owner applied it to Paul's hand.

"Thank you," said Paul, and to the other diners he said, "Please forgive us."

The hubbub that often follows a moment of crisis or shock, the immediate, frantic conversation that is pointedly resumed, now filled the silence; the Danish couple launched into earnest conversation, both talking at the same time, and volubly too; the elderly man said something more about hens, although he was not heard by the woman in the kitchen, who was talking loudly to the waiter.

Seated once more, Paul said to Gloria, "Let's pretend that didn't happen. Let's enjoy our dinner."

Gloria rolled her eyes. "How can you? You can't."

"Well, I can," said Paul. "You're simply wrong, Gloria."

"What's going to happen now?"

Paul shrugged. "Nothing. And I don't think there's anything I can do. I imagine she'll go home." He paused. "I'm sorry it's ending this way, but I suppose sometimes it does."

She looked at him. "I suppose you're right," she said. "I suppose that's the way affairs come to an end. Somebody grabs a fork and stabs the other in the hand. And that's it."

Paul sighed. "I'm going to have to go and see that she's all right. I can't leave her like that."

"I'm coming with you," said Gloria. "She could be dangerous."

"Nonsense. You stay. I'll be back in fifteen minutes. Start the meal. I'll catch up."

He would not listen to her protest, and he left. It was only five minutes' walk to the Fiore, where he imagined Becky would have returned. He suddenly realised that there was something that he had not said, that he now needed to say, to bring the whole matter to an end. He had never said sorry, which, curiously enough, is what the person who is in the wrong is often waiting for the wronged party to say.

He saw her in the hotel. She was weeping, but the quivering of her lip showed him that the tears were of remorse as much as anything else.

"I know you didn't mean it," he said. "And I also know that I should have said sorry a long time ago for . . . well, for everything. For not giving you enough of my time. For not thinking of you enough. For all of that."

She shook her head. "I was the one who . . ."

"No, listen to what I'm saying. I'm the one who's saying sorry now. And I think we both know that it's over, and that we need to get on with our lives. I don't want you to think that I hate you or anything."

"I don't want you to think that either," she sobbed. "I don't hate you either."

"Well, that's good, then." He paused. "Why don't you

come back and have dinner with us? You know, there's nothing between Gloria and me. There really isn't."

She shook her head. "I can't. And I'm going tomorrow."

"We could have breakfast. The Fiaschetteria. How about that?"

She wiped at her tears. "All right."

13

Don't Fall in Love with This Place

So," said Gloria at lunch the next day. "So that's that?"

"She felt very sorry about it," said Paul.

Gloria glanced at his hand. The plaster provided by the restaurant had been replaced with a neat square of dressing, held in position by two transparent strips. These had been purchased in the chemist's shop near the Fiore and applied by the chemist herself, who had inspected the wound and pronounced it inconsequential.

"How did you do it?" she asked as she squirted a fine antiseptic spray over Paul's hand.

"A fork," answered Paul.

The chemist peered more closely at the broken skin. "Most unusual, I must say. Mind you, we get everything in here. We had a man who bit his tongue in an argument with a neighbour. That sort of thing."

Now, sitting with Gloria at one of the outside tables of the Fiaschetteria, Paul reflected on the morning's events. He had breakfasted with Becky, who had repeated her apologies for what had happened the previous evening. "I'd never want to hurt you, Paul—you know that, don't you?"

He assured her that he did. "I hope we can be friends," he said.

"Yes, we can," she said. "You know something, Paul? I

haven't told you this before, but I will now. There was another reason why I came here. It wasn't just to say sorry to you."

He thought: *I knew it.*

But then, when she continued, it turned out to be something quite different. "Tommy and I had been going through a rough patch. I thought that he was taking me a bit for granted."

"Oh?"

"Yes. And so I thought that if I came out to see you, that might make him think about his position—might make him sit up and realise that there were alternatives."

Paul kept his voice level—with difficulty. "I see."

"And that worked, you know. It really worked. He's been bombarding me with messages, asking me to come back as soon as possible. He's suggesting we go off on holiday. He says that he's missing me terribly."

Paul heaved a sigh of relief. "I'm glad. In fact, I'm very happy for you, Becky."

"You know something," she continued. "I read somewhere that a bit of competition can really help a relationship from getting stale. I think that might have worked in this case."

Paul stared at her. Did I *ever* understand her? he thought.

"I'm sure you're very good for him, Becky. He's a lucky man."

"He's a nice guy," said Becky. "He's gentle. Strong men often are, aren't they?"

Paul thought about this. She was probably right. He remembered the school bully, who had been puny, but who used Japanese fighting skills to get his opponents off balance.

"I suppose I've got you out of my system now," said Becky, thoughtfully. "I know that sounds a bit rude—and I hope you don't take it the wrong way, but I think this trip has worked for me in more ways than one. It's shown I could never take you back."

Paul momentarily floundered. "Take me . . . take me back?"

"Yes," said Becky. "I don't think that it would work in the long term. We're different types, Paul, and we should have realised that a long time ago."

He thought she was right. "Yes, we are."

"Plenty of people go through their life with the wrong person," Becky continued. "They think they're suited, but they aren't. They even make a mistake about what sex of person they want. I know this woman who's been with this guy for years and only now realises that she wants to be with another woman. She's in her late forties. All that time wasted."

"Well, she found what she was looking for."

"She did. Tommy says life isn't a dress rehearsal."

"Oh, he says that, does he?"

"Yes. He says we should live for the moment."

Paul said that he thought Tommy was right.

"There's more to Tommy than meets the eye," observed Becky.

"Still waters run deep," replied Paul.

*B*ecky left for Siena on the eleven o'clock bus. Gloria moved into her vacated room an hour later, helped by a strangely silent Ella, who was clearly struggling to work out what was going on. Word had got out of the fork incident, which was the talk of the market that morning. By the time that Ella was making up the room for Gloria, the word was that there had been an attempted murder in the restaurant last night, with Paul being the victim of an onslaught with a steak knife, receiving injuries that required twenty-four stitches and an immediate transfusion of blood. The perpetrator, it was said, had fled the village—but had more or less definitely been arrested at Fiumicino Airport, trying to leave the country.

Gloria settled into her new room and into a routine in the town. She went for long walks, leaving Paul to work on the book; she bought a sketch book and began to pencil sketches of winding streets and hidden alleyways. Paul took her on the bulldozer to Sant'Antimo, where they heard the monks singing plainchant. She loved the bulldozer. "It's so ridiculous," she said. "In fact, it's utterly and completely absurd."

"Of course it is," said Paul. "But then why should we expect the world to be mundane and sensible?"

"It's just that people don't hire bulldozers," said Gloria. "They don't drive them around Tuscany. They just don't."

"They do," said Paul.

They made a picnic for themselves—rolls, salami, olives— and took it with them to a place they had found on one of their walks. It was a quiet place, a place of scattered oaks and, in the distance, a vineyard that climbed a gently sloping hillside until it joined the sky. She asked him about Anna.

"Where is she?" she said.

"I think she's spending a few days in Siena. She should be back soon. But I'm trying not to think about her."

Gloria closed her eyes. "That's probably a good idea." And then she asked, "Will I see her, do you think?"

"I don't think so."

He picked up a twig and began to strip off its bark. "I don't know about my life," he said. "I just don't know."

She half-opened her eyes. The sky was limitless, a singing, dizzying emptiness of blue. "What do you mean?" And then, before he could answer, "Does any of us know?"

"The sort of thing I do," he said. "What's the point? What difference do I make?"

"You mean, is what you do superficial? Is that your question?"

"In a way, yes. I've met people who are doing much more with their lives. Doctors, for instance. A couple of months ago I met a male nurse—a psychiatric nurse. He looks after people in their homes—he goes to check up on them, takes them out for walks, makes them feel better. What do I do? Write about mushrooms."

It took her a few moments to work out her reply. "You give pleasure to people. That's a perfectly good thing to do with your life."

He was sceptical. "Is it really?"

"Yes, it is. Look at artists. What do artists do?"

"Paint. Make us think. Show us beauty."

"You make us think. You show us beauty."

"Hardly."

"Yes, you do. There are various forms of artistry, Paul. The person who grows grapes and makes wine is an artist, I think. The person who writes about all that is also an artist."

He made a grudging admission. "Possibly."

They were both silent for a while. Then she said, "The problem is that you don't have a sense of your future."

"And we need that?"

"We do. We need to believe in something. For most of us that includes having some sense of where we're going."

"And I don't have that sense?"

"I don't think you do."

The twig was now bare. He looked at it closely and caught the sharp smell of sap. "I suppose I'll sort myself out. Eventually."

"There's a long tradition of coming to Italy to do that," said Gloria. "It's been a sort of rite of passage over the years. The North comes to the South to discover all about love and beauty. Poets, painters. They've all done that."

He dropped the twig. "And some never made it back."

"Some didn't."

It was time for them to start walking back to the town. Gloria was leaving the following day and they were to have dinner together one final time. On the way back, they said very little.

"You're not offended by what I said?" asked Gloria.

"Of course not. Why should I be?"

"Because what you do with your life is really no concern of mine. You don't need me to tell you what to do."

He did not think that friendship was of such limited compass. "I think we should tell our friends when we think they're not getting something right."

"You wouldn't hesitate to tell me if . . ."

"If I thought you were all over the place." He smiled. "I don't." He paused. "Although I suppose I could say something to you if I thought about it."

"And what would that be?"

"To let yourself go. Let yourself fall in love, perhaps. Not to be so—how shall I put it—so above it all."

She lowered her gaze, and he thought, *Now I've hurt her.*

"I'm sorry," he mumbled.

"No, it's all right."

He tried to make up for his tactlessness. "I'm sure that somebody's going to come along. Somebody who's going to sweep you off your feet."

"I'm not so sure, but that would be nice, I suppose."

He persisted. "It could happen."

She made light of it. "Unlikely. And anyway, it's not my feet that have to be prised from the ground—it's *his*." She added, "Whoever he is."

*H*e watched the bus drive down the road past the Rocca. He waved, and thought that he saw a hand at a window, waving back at him. It was a warm morning and the heat of the sun was heavy on the back of his neck. He felt curiously flat; he had enjoyed the last few days with Gloria, sharing in the pleasure of her discovery of Montalcino, showing his temporary home to her as a proud local might do. Now that she had gone it meant an end to the walks together, to the sheer pleasure of having the company of an old friend to whom one had nothing to explain, nothing to apologise for; an old friend, like a familiar set of clothes. From being embarrassed by her arrival, he had gone to being glad of it. And he was surprised to discover that during her stay he had barely thought of Anna, at least after he had confessed his interest in her to Gloria. He regretted that confession now, as one is always likely to regret revealing the secrets of the heart too freely. He was no longer sure how he felt; he liked the *idea* of Anna—she *was* attractive, her conversation *was* stimulating, but the idea of being in love with her seemed excessive. He was no longer an adolescent, ready to fall head over heels for somebody he barely knew. Or was he? Did we ever outgrow that stage? Was it as simple as that? You fell for a face, for a figure, for a way of walking or standing, prompted by a primal biological urge that somewhere or other along the line had become mixed up with a sense of beauty, so that the desire for beauty became the desire to possess another. That urge famously launched ships, inspired poetry, destroyed the most ordered lives, but at heart was something so simple and basic that its potency, viewed in the cold light of day, was absurd. And yet it existed, and none was immune to its Siren draw.

His desk awaited him, but Gloria had been both taskmaster and friend, and with her departure he felt freed of the claims of work. He would return to his manuscript later that day, but for now he would sit in the Fiaschetteria and simply watch the life of the town. He would order a coffee and think. He would let life happen to him rather than make it happen.

Onesto was there, but not by himself. Seated opposite him was a slightly younger man, dressed in clerical black, a tall glass of iced water in front of him. Spotting Paul, Onesto signalled for him to join them at their table.

"This is Father Stefano," said Onesto, as Paul sat down. "He is, as you'll see, a priest. He's actually *the* priest, although I am not one of his flock, being liberated from all that."

The priest grinned. "There is always a road back for you."

Onesto shook his head vigorously. "No thank you, Stefano. That road goes downhill as far as I'm concerned."

Paul made the connection. This was the Stefano to whom Tonio had referred; this was the younger brother.

"I believe I've met your brother, Tonio. I've been to his place."

This brought a quick exchange of glances between the other two men, and Stefano reddened slightly. "My brother, Tonio," he said quickly. "Yes, Onesto told me you had visited him. I go there quite often myself for meals. Tonio is a better cook than he lets on."

Paul remembered what Tonio had said about his wife having left him. "Your brother was married once, I believe."

Stefano nodded. "He was. She left him and went to live in Milan. I haven't seen her for years."

A look of anger came to Onesto's face. "Shameful," he said. "She went off with a communist, originally from Palermo. Bad wine, bad people."

"Oh, I don't know about their wine," said Stefano. "Not as good as ours, but hardly bad." He looked at Paul. "You'd agree, would you not, *dottore*?"

"I think I would," said Paul cautiously. "Some Sicilian wine is very good."

"But not the people," said Onesto.

"They are just people, same as anywhere," said Stefano. "We shouldn't condemn them just because of where they come from."

"But where you come from makes you what you are," argued Onesto. "If you're born in a stable, that makes you a horse."

"Our Lord was born in a stable," observed Stefano.

"I'm not talking about him," snapped Onesto. "I'm talking about Sicily."

Stefano made an effort to change the subject. "Your Italian is very good," he said. "We get few foreigners who speak it well. Nobody bothers to learn it because it is spoken only here and nowhere else."

"I like the language," said Paul. "I like the country."

"Don't fall in love with this place," said Onesto. "Italy is a seductress. Remember that."

Stefano gave Onesto a discouraging look. "You tasted my brother's wine, I take it?"

Paul smiled. "I did. And I thought it very good."

"It's Rosso di Montalcino, of course," continued Stefano. "That means he doesn't get the prices that Brunello attracts."

"Snobbery," said Onesto.

Stefano made a gesture of acceptance. "Perhaps, but the world is the way it is, I'm afraid."

Onesto crowed at this. "You say that, do you? You, of all people, Stefano! You say that the world is as it is and we just have to accept it. Then why are you dressed the way you are? Why do you tell people to pray that it gets better? Pray to what, I ask you? To the sky?"

"Our prayers are not to the sky," said Stefano quietly. "They are to . . ."

"Somebody who lives in the sky," interjected Onesto. "Up there, where Michelangelo painted him. Up there. Yes!"

Stefano smiled patiently, glancing at Paul as if to excuse his friend. "You have a very crude idea of what we believe, Onesto. You yourself believe very firmly in certain things— I know you do: human rights, reason, things like that—but you can't show me those, can you? You can't point to something that I can touch or feel and say, *That, you see, is Reason.* You can't do that, and yet you expect me to be able to show you God and say, *That, you see, is God.*"

Onesto turned to Paul. "You must forgive our theological argument. It is rude to argue about theology in the presence of others, but Stefano and I go back a long way and have talked about these matters ever since he went off to the Gregorian. I think he regards me as a project."

Stefano laughed. "There is no need for me to convert you to anything, Onesto. You are a good man, and in the eyes of God that is enough. His mercy is freely given to all."

"That's very condescending," Onesto said. "What if I don't want his mercy? What if I deny the existence of such a thing?"

Stefano ignored the challenge and pointed, instead,

through the door into the piazza outside. "Our friend from Florence. See."

Paul looked out into the square. A heavy-set man with a rather peevish expression was speaking intently to a smaller, bespectacled figure. A point was being driven home—strongly, thought Paul, in view of the gestures being made by the larger man.

"Ah, there he is," said Onesto. And to Paul he explained, "The big man—not the one in spectacles—is a very wealthy man from Florence. He is a property developer who bought a house here. He is very rarely here, even in the summer, but it's kept ready for him by a housekeeper who lives in it. He is a very arrogant man."

"He is certainly not humble," agreed Stefano.

"He built a wall recently," Onesto continued. "He walled off an orchard that local people liked to walk through. It was a very unpopular move. Not only did he prevent people walking where they had walked for a very long time, but he spoilt the view from the Casa di Riposa, the home for the old people. They used to sit on their balcony and look over the valley; after the wall, they couldn't."

Stefano spoke quietly. "No. But it's different now, isn't it?"

Onesto grinned. "It certainly is. His wall fell over one night. Miraculously. Suddenly people could walk in the orchard again and the old people could see the valley once more."

"A miracle," said Stefano.

Onesto's expression was hard to read. It was as if there was something he would like to say but could not. "There was a certain justice in what happened," he mused. "He built the wall against everybody's wishes."

Paul waited for further explanation. Stefano provided it.

"You need permission to build, you see—the days when you could build whatever you like are over. You have to go to the Commissione Edilizia and get their say-so. He didn't bother—he just built."

"Had he bothered," Onesto said, "the Commissione would have taken into account the community's objections. But, as it was, he just went ahead and did it."

Paul wondered whether there was any remedy: Could the Comune not simply order the demolition of an unapproved structure? He recalled somebody at home who had been obliged to lower a roof that had been built higher than the planners had authorised—could the same thing not happen here?

"In theory, yes," said Onesto. "But what he did was to raise a complicated legal appeal. If you want to slow things down in Italy, the answer is to have recourse to law. A very simple matter can take years to resolve. You delay proceedings; you come up with all sorts of pleas and counter-pleas; you appeal every interim decision, every procedural ruling; and you can tie things up for ten years or even more."

"He's right," said Stefano. "It would have taken at least that long to get a decision on that wall, and by then he would have been able to argue that the opposition had been withdrawn, and it would probably remain exactly where it is."

"Very cynical," said Onesto. "He's cynically used the system to overcome local opposition."

Stefano was smiling. "But, of course, everything is different now that the wall has collapsed. His contractor will have a court order slapped on him to prevent his building again. The Comune is alerted to him now—that's the Mayor he's talking to. But it won't do him any good."

"No good at all," agreed Onesto.

Paul was lost in thought. "What actually happened to the wall?" he asked. "Was it badly built? Was it unstable?"

"Oh, no," blurted out Stefano, "it was very well-constructed . . ." Onesto glanced at him, and he stopped. "I don't really know," he continued lamely. "It's a complete mystery."

"Exactly," said Onesto. "These things sometimes happen without any obvious explanation. Very odd indeed."

14

He's Loved Her All These Years

$\mathcal{P}$aul had imagined that it would be for him to contact Anna once she returned from Siena, but it was she who made the first move. This came in the form of a message left the following day—a Saturday—at the Fiore. Paul was taking a break from his manuscript and had wandered down to the car park to check on the bulldozer and discovered the note on his return. *May I invite you to a picnic?* she wrote. *I have no idea where to go, but I could get some things from the* alimentari *at the end of the road and you must know some places. Tomorrow? Here's my cell number.*

Going back up to his room, he dialled the number and stood at the window while the phone rang.

"I'm looking out of my window," he said when she answered. "Are you in your apartment?"

"I am."

"I'm not sure which is your window—can you wave to me?"

He looked down and across the hotel garden to the sloping roofs and the shaded walls. A shutter opened suddenly—not the one he had expected—and he saw her. She waved, and he returned her signal.

"It's very odd," he said. "Speaking to somebody on the phone when you can see them is just odd."

She moved inside. "Is that better?"

"You've been in Siena?"

"It was very successful—that's why I stayed a bit longer than I'd planned. But it's good to be back."

"Too hot down there?"

"Boiling. But the library I was working in was cool enough. Those old buildings keep the heat out."

"And the cold in during winter."

She laughed. "I suppose so. Mind you, I don't think of this place as having winter."

"It can get very cold." Onesto had told him that the previous winter had been particularly hard, coming early and all but ruining the olive crop.

"I assume you got my note," she said.

"I did. And a picnic's a great idea—since it'll be Sunday. Well, even if it weren't, it would still be a good idea."

He toyed with the idea of asking her whether she was free for dinner that evening, but he did not. He felt anxious, and did not want to crowd her. The rest of the conversation was about arrangements: she would get everything, she said, but he could perhaps choose a bottle of white wine, as she knew very little about what was available. Could he chill it in the fridge at the Fiore? He thought he could. And would they need to go by bulldozer?

"I feel so silly asking that question," she said. "I still can't get over the fact that you have a bulldozer."

He laughed. "Nor can I. Sometimes I think it's a weird dream and that I'll wake up, but then I see my bulldozer and I realise that it actually exists. But no, we won't go by bulldozer—we can walk."

They ended the conversation—reluctantly, he thought, on both sides—and for a moment he remained where he was, looking down towards her window. He had been unaware of it during the conversation, but now he felt his heart thumping hard within him. It was sheer and simple excitement— the feeling that precedes a meeting with a lover, or somebody one hopes will become a lover. He closed his eyes. Was that what he wanted?

He moved back from the window and lay down on his bed, staring up at the ceiling above him. His eye slipped down to the wall directly behind him, and stopped at a tiny red mark, like a teacher's red tick on the page of an exercise book. Somebody had swatted a mosquito at that precise spot, too late, as the mosquito had already drawn blood. He had heard a mosquito the night before, an insistent drone like that of a tiny night fighter, and he had buried his head under the sheet in order to protect himself. But they always found some small landing place of skin and got what they were looking for.

He closed his eyes. *Why am I doing this? Why am I bothering about somebody who has her own life? We won't see one another again after this, even if . . .* For a moment he imagined himself with her, and the thought filled him with need. It could happen, and he wanted it to happen. And why not? Why should he be ashamed of his yearning for tenderness, for love?

He stood up and made a deliberate effort to put such thoughts out of his mind. Between now and the picnic there were eighteen hours—eighteen hours to get through somehow without . . . absurd thought, exploding. But that was what it's like, he thought. That's what being in love is like. It's like waiting for something terribly important to happen; it's like being on the edge of something; it's like hearing loud chords of Bach resonating in some great cathedral; it's like surfing a giant wave, being carried, barrelled along by the roaring watery creature beneath one.

No, he thought. It can't be. She has somebody else and she's simply being friendly. There is no point—no point at all.

Somehow he made it to eleven o'clock that Sunday morning. The nearby church bells were ringing out over the roofs of the houses, while in the distance, from another tower somewhere far below, came a faint answering toll, audible only because there was a breeze from that direction. He had bought a bottle of wine the previous evening—a light Tuscan wine, a Vermentino from the coast. He had just finished a section of his book in which he talked about the coastal wines and their special qualities. He had talked about *sapidità,* and had tried, unsuccessfully, to translate the word to convey the taste of the grape variety. He would leave it at that: *sapidità* would remain just that, just as those who are *simpatico* could remain untranslated.

She had suggested that he call round for her. She had a rucksack, she said, in which they could carry the food and there would be room for his bottle of wine. "We can wrap it in newspaper to keep it cool," she said.

He counted the minutes and was there at exactly eleven. A piece of paper had been taped above one of the two door bells: *Appleton.* Her name. Anna Appleton. AA. It was perfect. *Thoughts on Florentine Painting of the Quatrocento* by Anna Appleton. Or *Raphael Revealed* by Anna Appleton.

She came to the door. She was every bit as attractive as he remembered; even more so. There was a brilliance to her now; a sort of light, like one of the women in those paintings of hers. Light from the street and sky, across her face, against the darkness of the small hallway behind her; an effect of *chiaroscuro,* as she would say.

"You're very punctual," she said.

He laughed nervously. "I always am. I've never missed a train in my life."

"That's good. I miss them all the time."

He saw that the rucksack was on the floor behind her. He noticed that she was wearing hiking boots—a sensible decision, even if they would be on paths all the time. "Ready?"

She nodded. "I am. And Andrew will be down in two seconds. He was doing something with his camera—putting in a memory card, I think. He takes very high definition photos and they use all . . ."

He did not hear the rest, but when she stopped he found himself saying, "Of course." And then, after a brief and painful silence—painful for him at least—he asked her when Andrew had arrived. "I didn't think he'd be here yet," he said.

"He arrived yesterday," she said. "He's four days early. He managed to get an extra few days' holiday."

"That's wonderful."

"Yes. It means that we can take a few days to go to Florence. And Verona, too—Andrew says that he's always wanted to see Verona. He loves opera. I'm trying to get tickets to *Aida.*"

He said, "Live elephants?" but without enthusiasm.

"I wish."

He heard a door close somewhere within and then Andrew appeared.

She stood aside to let them shake hands. "This is Andrew," she said. "And this is Paul."

Paul reached out and took the other man's hand. He met his eyes; he saw the large red-wine-stain birthmark across the forehead. He saw that it extended down to the right eyebrow to end just above the eye. He flinched. He could not help it, and it must have been felt in his handshake as Andrew increased the pressure exerted by his own hand.

Anna took control of the situation. "That's us all ready," she said briskly. "Paul knows where we're going, don't you Paul?"

He collected himself. "Yes, I do." His voice was too loud. He lowered it. "There's a path down the hillside at the other end of the village. You go about two miles—maybe a bit more—and you get to an oak wood. They hunt for truffles there, I'm told, but it's a great place for a picnic."

"And no wild boars?" asked Andrew. "I was reading that this place is teeming with wild boars."

"Oh, they're there," said Paul. "But they won't bother us. They keep out of the way."

He noticed Andrew's diction, and his accent too. He spoke precisely, articulating each word deliberately, with a touch of Irish; Boston, of course.

The bottle of wine was tucked into the rucksack. "I'll carry," said Andrew. "You're the guide. The guide travels light."

Paul glanced as Andrew shouldered the rucksack. He was not a large man, and was perhaps even fractionally shorter than Anna, who was on the tall side. He was not what Paul had expected; he had imagined somebody of sporting appearance, some ruggedly handsome product of an Ivy League university, somebody with the confidence—if not the arrogance—of the Greek gods who peopled the financial firms of Boston and New York. Andrew was not that.

They set off. As they passed the Fiaschetteria, he saw Onesto standing in the doorway, talking to the owner. There was a cheerful wave, which Paul reciprocated. Along the road, they stopped briefly at a tobacconist while Andrew went in to purchase stamps for postcards. Paul and Anna waited outside.

"How long have you and Andrew known one another?" Paul asked.

She glanced into the shop. "Since we were sixteen."

"At high school together?"

She nodded. "Yes. We were at different colleges, and we didn't see one another for a while, but we got together a few years out of college. Then he went to work in Frankfurt and we didn't really see one another for some time. Not until he came back to the States."

"So it's been on and off?"

"Yes. But now . . ." She did not finish the sentence. "It hasn't been easy for Andrew, you know."

He was not sure what she meant. "You mean . . ."

"I mean life hasn't been easy. People don't realise how hard it is if you have something like that." She looked directly into his eyes. "You know what I'm talking about. His birthmark. People draw back. They're embarrassed. You were, weren't you?"

He was flustered. "I suppose . . ."

"Yes, but I don't blame you for it. I should have said something in advance."

"That wasn't necessary."

"It still takes people by surprise. They don't know where to look."

She looked into the shop again. Andrew had paid for his stamps and was coming out, tucking a small packet into the pocket of his shirt. He looked at Paul and smiled. "I reached the limit of my Italian," he said.

They were soon on the path that led from the village, edging their way slowly down the steeper sections. The sun, approaching its zenith, made shadows short and intense; there was the thrum of cicadas, the sound, it had always seemed to Paul, of heat. They passed the church where Paul had stopped a few days earlier, but now, in company, he felt none of the unease he had experienced when he had been there on his own.

"I was here the other day," he said. "There was something odd about that church. I felt really uneasy for some reason. I think there was somebody there."

"Sometimes old churches have that feeling," said Anna. "I know what you mean."

"It's because they're old," said Andrew.

"But everything is in Italy," said Paul. "And that church is probably only a couple of hundred years old."

He had not intended to be cutting, but he realised after he had spoken that he had sounded dismissive. Anna said quickly, "This is Andrew's first visit to Italy."

Paul bit his tongue. He glanced at Andrew, who was blushing.

"I'm sorry," said Paul. "I wasn't being sarcastic."

Andrew made light of it. "I didn't think you were. It's okay."

They continued their walk and came at last to the oak wood and the place that Paul had thought would be suitable for the picnic. They sat down and Paul uncorked the bottle of wine while Anna cut slices from a salami and Andrew tipped olives from a jar onto a paper plate.

Paul dispensed the wine. The newspaper had kept the bottle chilled and now the cold liquid brought condensation to the sides of the small plastic glasses. Paul raised his to the others. Anna put the salami aside and raised her glass in response. "To your book," she said.

"And to yours," said Paul.

He looked at Andrew, and saw that the other man was gazing at Anna. *He loves her,* he thought. *He's loved her all these years.* He glanced at Anna, and just as he did so, she looked up, met his gaze, and something passed between them. And that thing was a current of sexual attraction. There was no mistaking it. It cannot be mistaken once it has been experienced. Nothing needed to be said; nothing needed to be done. It just occurred.

She looked away. She reached for the plate of salami she had been preparing and hurriedly moved the slices over to one side of the plate, using her knife. Paul said, "Can I help you with that?"

She said no, she was fine and would cut just a little bit more salami. If anybody wanted extra, they could always help themselves.

Andrew took a sip of his wine. He was looking up at the sky. He said, "Gee, that sky . . . look at it."

"Makes me dizzy," said Anna.

Paul raised his glass to his lips. Plastic made wine taste cheap, he thought—even a good wine like this.

Andrew said, "I'm going to go and take a look at the thing over there. What is it?"

He pointed to a small stone structure, about the size of a small hut, at the edge of the wood.

"It's a shrine," said Paul. "You may find a Madonna in it."

He walked off. Paul turned to Anna and said, "I like him."

She said nothing for a moment. Then she turned and looked at the retreating figure. "I'm all he has," she said.

Paul was silent. "He obviously needs you."

"He does."

Paul felt his breath coming quickly. "I don't think it would be a good idea," he said.

She frowned. "What?"

"If you and I were to get closer." He said it without thinking, and now he realised that it was a remark that could not be taken back.

She stared at him. "No, I think you're right."

"I'm sorry about that," he said.

Her voice was very quiet although there was nobody to hear them. "And so am I," she said.

He was silenced by the immensity of what he had said, and by the effect it had produced. It was as if he had suddenly confessed his inmost thoughts to a complete stranger; and that, in a way, was what had happened. He barely knew her; he had seen her how many times—three or four—and yet he had effectively told her that he had recognised in her the same desire that he nurtured within himself. And he had done this while the man to whom she was clearly committed had his back turned.

He felt grubby; he felt ashamed; and she must too, he suspected.

Andrew was on his way back now. "You're right," he said. "It was a shrine. There was a Madonna and some flowers. Somebody had put flowers there."

"The farmer," said Paul. "Or truffle hunters perhaps. You don't see them, but these woods are full of people."

"I love that," mused Andrew. "I love it that there should be this little shrine in the middle of nowhere. And that a plaster statue can be left there quite safely."

"Nobody would steal the Virgin Mary," said Paul.

"I guess they wouldn't," said Andrew. "It would be like destroying something innocent—something good."

Which is what I've almost done, thought Paul. And then he thought: *Am I any worse than anybody else? Would any man do the same? Is that how people behave?*

Anna gave them each a plate with bread, salami, olives, and a hunk of Parmesan cheese. She avoided looking at Paul, and he at her. But she spoke to him.

"Piero di Cosimo," she said. "I went to Florence for the afternoon with one of the people from the library in Siena. There was a di Cosimo exhibition at the Uffizi."

Paul squeezed the residual brine out of an olive. He did not like too much salt. "Which one was he?" Casual conversation would cover the things underneath.

"The one who painted that dog." That was Andrew. "That right, Anna?"

"Yes, the dog. The dog is looking on, I suppose; it's really about the young woman being mourned by the satyr."

Andrew grinned. "I pick things up," he explained to Paul. "When you're with somebody for a long time, you pick things up. I can go on for hours about the Ghirlandaios and Michele Tosini. Not that I do." He turned to Anna. "What did you say that painting meant?"

Paul glanced at her quickly, and saw that the question had appeared to make her feel uncomfortable.

"I don't think I said anything special," Anna muttered.

Andrew seemed surprised. "But you did. I saw the photograph of it—on your desk. You had been discussing it with your students. Something about jealousy." He paused. "Wasn't there a play or a poem. That guy Ovid."

Anna laughed. "That guy Ovid! Really, Andrew . . ."

"I know who you mean," said Paul.

"Andrew may be a fund manager," said Anna, now looking at Paul. "But he actually has a degree from Dartmouth. He's encountered that guy Ovid. And that guy Virgil."

Paul said nothing.

"Do you know how peculiar di Cosimo was?" Anna went on. "He led a very eccentric life. You know that Vasari said of him, 'He could not bear the crying of babies, the coughing of men, the sound of bells, and the chanting of friars.'"

Andrew remembered something. "And didn't you say something about boiled eggs?"

"He lived on them," said Anna. "Or so Vasari tells us. He boiled whole batches of them when he was boiling his glue— fifty, sixty at a time—and then ate them while he worked."

Paul poured more wine into each glass. The Vermentino was going to his head, but it had dispelled the feeling of mortification that had followed upon his disclosure of his feelings. He threw a glance at Anna, and she smiled at him. It was doing the same for her. They were friends. Something strange, something disturbing and wrong, had been dispatched, consigned to an area of quarantine somewhere deep within, but no longer dangerous or disturbing.

They did not linger over their picnic. Clouds had built up in the distance, and were now moving across the sky towards them; heavy cumulus clouds, grey and purple. The wind that brought them smelled of rain, that unmistakeable, dusty smell that tickles the back of the nose.

"We need to get back," said Paul. "Unless we want a soaking."

Anna did not seem to care, but Andrew was becoming anxious. "I don't like lightning," he said.

"I know why you don't," said Anna. "Remember Mr. Humphrey, the chemistry teacher?"

Andrew explained to Paul. Mr. Humphrey had been struck by lightning on a golf course. "It really affected us when we were kids," he said. "Some people wouldn't go out if there was any sign of a storm. It had a big effect."

"He was such a nice man, too," said Anna. "There were other teachers who deserved it more than he did. That's what we thought."

"Lightning's no judge of character," offered Paul.

They packed up the detritus of the picnic—the empty bottle, the wrapping of the salami, the half-full olive jar—and began to retrace their steps. On the way back, at the point where they began to climb the side of the hill, they were met by a figure coming down the path. They rounded the corner and he was there before them, carrying a large plastic bag of the sort provided by supermarkets.

The priest stopped when he saw them. He seemed to hesitate, as if debating with himself as to whether to continue, but they were just a few paces from one another and an encounter could not be avoided.

"Father Stefano," said Paul. "The storm . . ."

Stefano looked up at the sky. "No, this won't be a proper storm. It's going to blow over. It probably won't even reach us."

Paul introduced the others. "These are my friends," he said.

Stefano switched to English, and shook hands.

"You're going for a walk?" asked Paul. He was puzzled by the bag; through its open mouth he had glimpsed a small loaf of bread and what looked like a wrapped cheese.

Stefano nodded. "Yes. Down there." He pointed vaguely towards the floor of the valley.

Paul's glance at the bag was intercepted. "For a parishioner," mumbled Stefano.

"Of course."

They said goodbye, and resumed their journey.

"That's an odd place to meet a priest," said Anna.

"Yes," said Paul. "It is."

He was thinking: bread, cheese.

15

How Rich Life Was

*H*e saw them on a couple of occasions after that. He passed them once on his way to the Fiaschetteria, and exchanged greetings. Andrew suggested they meet for a drink one evening, and he accepted, although he thought they would not have time. And then they were off to Verona: tickets for *Aida* had become available at the last minute, and they were to drive there in Andrew's rental car.

There was nothing in Anna's demeanour to indicate any regret, and Paul was relieved by that. For his part, he felt as if a hidden well of feeling had been drained, and now there was friendship, a certain warmth, but nothing more. It had been, he decided, one of those odd moments when we see a beguiling face and are momentarily seized by the thought of what might be—a sudden yearning, a moment of temptation, that, not surprisingly, is rarely capable of being anything more.

When they left for Verona, Paul realised that he had only a few days left in Montalcino. He had worked hard, and there were ten pages left to write before the manuscript would be finished. He had the material for these ready, and the writing of them would not take long. He sent an e-mail to Gloria, which said, *Within a whisker of finishing. Then I'm coming back. Missing you. P.* He had written *Missing you* without thinking. He was about to delete it, but then he thought, *I am missing her. I am.* He left the message as it was and waited for her reply. Gloria was famous for responding quickly to e-mail, and her message flashed back within minutes. *Missing you too,* she wrote.

He finished the book two days before he was due to leave. There would be a bit of rewriting to do later on, once Gloria had edited the manuscript, but his task was effectively over. He rose from his work table. He had been sitting at it from six that morning, and it was now ten. He stretched, and closed his eyes. Finished.

He went out, pausing to tell Ella as he left that his labours were over.

"You've worked so hard," she said. "Just like a German."

He made his way to the Fiaschetteria, feeling almost light-headed. It was a bright morning, and although it would get hot later on, a cool breeze kept the heat at bay. He took deep breaths, savouring the scents of the village—the whiff of baking, the heavy scent of the nasturtiums in the window boxes, the smell of stone from the buildings around him.

Onesto and Stefano were in the café. They greeted him warmly, inviting him over.

"I've finished my book," Paul announced. "Ten minutes ago."

"An entire book!" exclaimed Onesto.

"Yes. My entire book. Finished—in time."

"*Complimenti, complimenti, complimenti!*" chanted Onesto. "I haven't even *started* my book yet."

"Your book?" enquired Stefano. "Onesto, you didn't say you were writing a book."

"Every village schoolteacher is writing a book," said Onesto. "In his head at least."

"It's only a book about food and wine," said Paul.

Onesto would not have the achievement underplayed. "It is nonetheless a book," he said. "That's the important thing." He stopped, as if an idea had just occurred to him. "We must celebrate this."

"I'm leaving the day after tomorrow."

Stefano frowned. "On your bulldozer?"

Paul shook his head. He had had a telephone call at the Fiore yesterday from the rental firm in Pisa. There was somebody needing a bulldozer in Pienza, and it would be much more convenient for them if one of their men could come to drive it the short distance over there. They would arrange a car to take him back to Pisa. "It will be more comfortable for you," the manager said. "And it will cost you nothing."

Over coffee, Paul explained all this to Stefano and Onesto, who exchanged glances with one another.

"Then you must join us for lunch tomorrow," said Stefano. "We are going to my brother's place."

"But I'm not invited."

"He'll be very happy to see you. It will be no problem for there to be one extra place at the table."

Onesto seconded the invitation. It was vital, he said, that Paul should come with them. He could not leave Montalcino without a proper celebration of the finishing of the book—that would be unthinkable.

"And would it be all right for us to travel down there on your bulldozer?" asked Stefano. "My own car is very unreliable these days."

"And mine is being used by my wife," said Onesto hastily. "She has gone to Montepulciano for the day. Her sister lives there."

Rather liking the thought of a final trip on the bulldozer, Paul agreed to this.

"Twelve o'clock tomorrow?" said Onesto. "Down at the car park?"

Onesto was expected at home, and excused himself. Paul half-rose, as if to go himself, but was urged by Stefano to stay. "Don't hurry away. Your book is written."

Paul sat back in his seat, and Stefano ordered a further coffee for each of them. He shifted in his seat, and it seemed to Paul that he was about to raise some awkward topic. Eventually he spoke. "You were kind to my brother," he said.

"He was kind to me," said Paul. "He gave me a very fine lunch."

"He is a good cook—he always was, but no, it's not about that. From what he told me, I can tell that you listened to him with kindness. I am very grateful."

Paul made a dismissive gesture. "It was nothing."

Stefano shook his head. "No, it was something very important. You see, my brother is sometimes ridiculed by people. Particularly because of his name."

"Yes, I had heard of that."

"And you were probably aware that it was invented. He really shares my name: Poggio."

Paul said that perhaps it meant something to him. "A lot of people are fascinated by these genealogical matters. It doesn't do much for me, but there are many who take a close interest in it."

"That's good of you to say that," said Stefano, "but in my brother's case it goes much deeper. He doesn't do it lightly."

"I didn't think he did," said Paul.

"You see, there's a reason," continued Stefano. He hesitated before leaning forward and saying, in not much more than a whisper, "There's a very personal reason. I do not wish to burden you with it, but I feel it's important you know."

"If you wish to tell me, it would be no burden," said Paul.

The priest looked around him; they could not be over-heard. "My brother is really my half-brother. We share a mother, but my father was not his father. When my mother married my father back in 1960, she was already pregnant—by another man. My mother was sixteen at the time, and she had a part-time position in a villa down towards Grosseto. She was a chambermaid. This villa was owned by a man who had very low morals. He paid attention to my mother—and . . ." He lowered his voice, so low now that Paul had to strain to catch what he was saying. "Those relations were not entirely consensual. He took advantage of my mother."

Paul caught his breath. "I'm very sorry," he said.

"Thank you. Now, the fact that it was non-consensual could have made it a criminal matter, but things were different in those days. Firstly, how can you prove that the woman has not consented? That's a very difficult thing to do—sometimes impossible."

Paul inclined his head. He was conscious of being admitted to some very deep family secret. The priest was choosing his words carefully, but it was clear what he was talking about.

"People did not dare to stand up for themselves," Stefano went on, "and in those days, in Italy, people often ended up blaming the woman. Stigma, you see. So a woman in that position would be looked at as somehow responsible for what happened, so to speak. It's shocking, but that was how it was.

"My father married her anyway, because he was worried he would never find a suitable wife and here was someone ready and willing. He knew that she was expecting a child, but he did it anyway. So my brother believed that he was his father—or did so until he was thirteen. And then a terrible thing happened—one of the boys at school, a brute of a boy, a bully, overheard his parents talking about it. They had heard of it through the villa staff, one of whom had witnessed something taking place. The bully told my brother all about it.

"He took it very badly. I think his whole idea of who he was was disturbed. Eventually, when he was about sixteen or seventeen, he tried to find his real father. He went down there and discovered that the villa was now owned by somebody altogether different. His father—his real father, that is—had gone down to Rome.

"My brother went down there and found that his father had just died. That was when he first conceived the idea of changing his name. But he waited until after my father's death."

Paul gave a start of surprise. "But why? Why on earth take the name of the man who had done that to your mother?"

Stefano sighed. "He thought that was who he was. It was important to him, you see, because my father, I'm afraid to say, had always rejected him. He was always cold towards Tonio. He regarded him, I suppose, as the product of . . . well, I suppose one way of putting it is as the product of sin." Stefano looked at Paul. "I imagine you might not use that word yourself. Do you?"

Paul shrugged. "Not really. But the equivalent exists—not that I'd use it in a situation like that. How can the circumstances of somebody's conception make the slightest difference to the person himself?"

"Oh, you don't need to tell me that," said Stefano. "And the Church herself make no judgements these days, anyway." He took a sip of his coffee. "Don't attribute to us the attitudes of the past. We've changed, you know."

Paul sat quite still. He imagined the young Tonio's feelings. If the man who was overtly his father did not want him, then who was he? "And all the time he was just trying to . . ."

"To assert his identity," supplied Stefano. "To establish who he was. He was struggling to find his place in the world."

"Which all of us feel the need to do," said Paul.

"That's right. But in the case of my poor brother it was much stronger a need than it is for most people. And, in a sense at least, that's what he's done. He belongs to that other family even if they have never even been aware of him. He belongs here too, but people have been unkind to him because he's a bit eccentric and mutters to himself—that sort of thing. But he's very gentle, you know—very kind. He would never harm a soul."

They sat in silence for a few minutes. Paul was going over in his mind what had been said to him. At last he spoke. "So your brother has had a hard life."

"Yes, he has."

Paul sighed. "Imagine being made to think that there's something fundamentally wrong with you. That you're *wrong* in some way. In your very being, your essence. That must have been how he felt, I suppose."

Stefano nodded his agreement. He hesitated, and then went on, "Precisely. And so many people have had that experience. Very many. People among us. Have felt guilty about themselves."

Paul looked at the priest, and suddenly he understood. Or perhaps he did not. That was what Italy was like; it was a palimpsest—there were layers and layers of meaning, just as there were centuries upon centuries of history, and beginning to understand it would take a lifetime.

·   ·   ·

*I*t was a tight fit for the three of them, but Onesto and Stefano perched on the spare seat and were able to hold on firmly enough to the bars protecting the top of the cab.

"We're perfectly comfortable," said Onesto as Paul started the engine. "This is my first time on a bulldozer, you know."

"And you?" Paul asked Stefano.

The priest hesitated. "Once before," he said at last.

"I have complete confidence in you," said Onesto. "Let's go."

As they made their way down the Grosseto road, Onesto gave a running commentary on the passing landscape. "That's where my uncle had a vineyard," he said, pointing to a small turning off the road. "He sold it before Brunello really took off. He'd be rich if only he'd held on to it."

"There were many in that position," said Stefano.

"And over there," continued Onesto. "That's where they hid food in a cave when the Germans were here. My grandfather told me about it. It was stacked with hams and cheeses because the occupying forces took everything they could lay their hands on. The Germans never found where the food was hidden."

Stefano looked away. "So much has happened in this country," he said. "It would be good to have a little less history."

"You can't change the past," said Onesto.

"No," conceded Stefano, "but you can make up for it, can't you?"

Onesto could not resist a dig. "Not that the Church does much of that."

Stefano ignored this. They were nearing the entrance to Tonio's vineyard. As they passed the sign with its elaborate crest, Onesto said, "Quite a crest, that. You must be pretty proud of it, Stefano."

"It's nothing to do with me," said Stefano calmly. "Some things are more important to my brother than they are to me." He paused. "But he remains my brother."

Paul parked the bulldozer where he had left it on his previous visit, and the three of them walked up to the villa. When Tonio appeared, he embraced Stefano first, and then turned to shake hands with Onesto and Paul, greeting them both with warmth.

"Stefano told me this is a celebration for you," he said, glancing over Paul's shoulder to where the bulldozer was parked. "A celebration and a farewell, I believe."

"I've finished my work," said Paul. "And I wrote a bit about your place and your wine. I assure you I've been complimentary."

"That is very kind of you," said Tonio.

They went inside, where Tonio had prepared an elaborate lunch. Wine was served out of a silver jug. Paul sipped at his slowly, aware of his driving duties, but he noticed that Onesto and Stefano were less restrained. As the lunch progressed, the conversation became increasingly uproarious. If there had been needling between Onesto and Stefano earlier on, this now all vanished, and the talk avoided any difficult or contentious subjects. There were reminiscences from school-days, discussion of the forthcoming boar hunt, and a long debate on the relative archery skills of the young men of the various *quartieri.*

At one point, while Stefano and Tonio were discussing some point of wine-making, Onesto turned to Paul and said, "They caught him, you know. Last night."

"Caught him?"

"That fugitive from justice. Occhidilupo. They caught him

in a bar down in the valley. He obviously thought he could slip in unrecognised, but the barman had seen his photograph and called the Carabinieri."

Stefano broke off his conversation with his brother. "I heard that too. My housekeeper was told by her brother in the Carabinieri."

"Well, they won't let him go so readily next time," said Onesto.

"He might be innocent," said Stefano quietly.

"Not him!" Onesto mocked.

"He was never actually convicted of anything," said Stefano. "Or not recently. Maybe a long time ago. But then he was judged thereafter. He was an outcast."

"Outlaw," corrected Onesto.

"Outcast," repeated Stefano.

Something came to Paul's mind. *As you are to the least of my brethren . . .* He spoke the words, and Stefano looked up sharply. He stared at Paul.

"Yes," he said.

Tonio produced the next course.

"You could write about a meal like this," said Onesto.

"Perhaps I shall," replied Paul.

Tonio rose from the table to fetch another bottle of wine, but came back with two.

"Don't worry," he said, as he drew the corks. "I'm not going to ask you to drink all of this. Just a small glass of each. A mouthful—no more. You'll need two glasses—one for each." He retrieved fresh glasses from a cupboard and distributed them round the table. Next he carefully poured all of them a small amount of wine from each bottle. The bottles, Paul noticed, had no labels.

"Now," said Tonio, looking directly at Paul. "Please taste both of them. Take as long as you like."

Paul raised the first glass, swirled the wine around in it, and held the glass up to the light to observe the colour. Then he took a small sip from each glass.

Tonio watched him closely. "Now, may I ask you: Which is the Brunello?"

Paul repeated his tasting. "This one," he said, tapping one of the glasses.

Tonio's face broke into a smile. "No," he said. "That is my Rosso di Montalcino. The other one is the Brunello, from the vineyard, as it happens, of one of the committee members of the Consorzio."

Hearing this, Stefano and Onesto began to laugh.

"I can just see their faces," said Onesto.

More wine was offered, but Paul declined. He felt relaxed—that was all—whereas the others looked and sounded ebullient.

"We have a small favour to ask," Stefano said suddenly. "Would you be able to help my brother with something?" He glanced at Tonio, who nodded encouragement.

Paul imagined it would be a further mention—perhaps in a newspaper article. "I'd do my best."

"Good," said Stefano. "Your bulldozer . . ."

Paul looked blank.

Tonio took up the explanation. "I need a mound of earth to be moved. It's quite big, but a bulldozer like that would do the task easily. Perhaps half an hour or so? An hour at the most."

Paul shrugged. "You'll have to show me."

"Oh, we'll do that, all right," said Tonio. "Stefano will ride in the cab. I'll direct from the ground."

"This is a great idea," said Onesto. "You're a very generous man, Paul. You must come back to Italy soon."

They went outside. Paul and Stefano climbed up into the cab while Tonio and Onesto walked off towards the beginning of the rows of vines.

"You see that big mound over there?" called Tonio, pointing to a small hillock. "We need to move that to the other side of the vines."

Paul gasped. "But that's massive "

"It's not small," conceded Stefano. "But it's clear ground between where it is now and where we want it. It won't be hard just to push the earth across." He paused. "That's what bulldozers do, isn't it?"

"But why?" asked Paul. "What's the point?"

"I'll tell you later," said Tonio. "You did say you'd help."

"Well, I did, but . . ."

"I can tell you: there is a reason. There really is."

Paul sighed. "I'm not sure if I really know how to do this sort of thing," he said. "But, all right, I'll try."

*I*t took longer than an hour, but at last, after a great deal of shouting and waving from Tonio and Onesto, and advice from Stefano, Paul scraped the last of the earth into its new position.

"A job well done," shouted Onesto.

"Magnificent!" decided Tonio. "Now we can go inside and celebrate."

The bulldozer was returned to its parking place, and Paul followed the other three into the house. Tonio went to a cupboard and took out a fresh bottle of wine. "This is something very special," he said. "You see the vintage? That was a very good year for us. I have only five or six bottles of it left."

He placed the bottle on the table. Stefano picked it up, looked at it, and whispered something to Onesto that Paul did not catch. Onesto smiled, and then laughed. Taking a pen out of his pocket, he crossed something out on the label and wrote something else in its place. He showed this to Tonio, whose eyes shone with pleasure.

"Here," said Onesto, passing the bottle to Paul for inspection.

Paul read what had been written. *Rosso di Montalcino* had been printed on the label, under Tonio's crest. Now, beneath those crossed-out words, was written *Brunello di Montalcino.*

"I told you I'd explain," said Stefano. "You see, the boundary of the Brunello zone of production runs right along the edge of my brother's vineyard. We've always felt that it was unfairly drawn, but would they listen to us?" He shook his head. "Now, the boundary was marked by an imaginary line drawn between a small hillock"—he paused to allow his words to sink in—"and the top of a hill over towards Sant'Angelo in Colle. So now that hillock is in—how shall we put this—a more advantageous position. If you draw that line now, it means that my brother's vineyard is in the Brunello zone of production."

"Hah!" said Tonio. "That'll teach them. I'll tell them that there's been a bad mistake and they should consult their records. I'll get the Comune surveyor to come out and confirm. Hah!"

He lifted a glass. "To you, *dottore*! And to our new Brunello!"

Paul raised his glass, too overcome by astonishment—and

emotion—to speak. And even if he could speak, what was there to say?

Later, on their way back to Montalcino, Stefano said to him, "That was a very good thing you did back there."

"It was hardly my idea," said Paul.

Onesto joined in. "No, but you were the one who did it." He paused. "Sometimes, you know, good things have to be done—they just have to be done. And most of us—myself included—are too timid to do them. Fortunately, there are brave people who are prepared to take the risk, who do these things, often in such a way that nobody can see them. They say, *The world doesn't have to be the way it is; we can change it.* That's what they say—and then they do it."

Paul saw that Onesto was looking at Stefano as he said this, but Stefano looked away.

*T*he bulldozer was collected the next morning by the man from Pisa. The man who had brought him was to drive Paul to the airport in time to catch his flight later that day. Onesto and Stefano came to say goodbye. They all watched the bulldozer be driven off, and then Paul loaded his luggage.

"There are permanent goodbyes and there are temporary ones," said Onesto, embracing him. "And this is a temporary one, I think, my dear friend."

"Thank you," said Stefano. "You have been good to us in more ways than you know."

Paul smiled at him. "And you have been good to me in the same way."

For a few moments he held Stefano's gaze, which was bemused, and then he got into the car and closed the door.

"It is always hard to leave friends," said the driver, as he started the engine.

"Very hard," said Paul.

Stefano stepped forward before the car drew away and tapped on Paul's window. Paul wound it down.

"I don't like to give advice," said Stefano. "Even if people expect me to do so because I am a priest."

Paul looked up at him, and smiled. "Tell me," he said.

"Follow your heart," said Stefano. "It's the best compass there is."

That night he and Gloria had dinner together in a small restaurant near Paul's flat. He had sent her a message from Montalcino, that morning—an important message. She had replied, although he did not get the message until his plane had touched down and he was waiting for his luggage. It simply read, *Of course.*

He had been puzzled, but now it seemed to him that things were clearer. "Do I detect your hand in what happened?" he asked. And then he added, "You don't need to tell me if you don't want to."

She tried to affect an innocent expression, but failed. "I'm such a bad liar," she said. "So I suppose I'm going to have to say yes. Not in everything, of course, but in some of it."

Paul nodded. He was still unsure why Becky had come out to see him. "Is it really possible to be so confused about one's feelings?"

"Yes," said Gloria, simply. "It is."

"So she really did want to apologise?"

"Yes, she did. She had been feeling pretty guilty."

"How do you know?" asked Paul.

Gloria hesitated. "You won't be cross with me?"

"Not if you tell me."

"Because she actually told me. She came to see me, and it

all spilled out. She was in a complete spin. And then she asked me whether I thought she should come out to say sorry in person—to explain herself."

"And what did you say?"

"I'm afraid I said yes. In fact, I rather encouraged her."

"Why?"

"Because I wanted to bring matters to a head. I was worried, you see, that when you came back you might just . . . well, you might fall right back into it. I thought that if she came out to Montalcino when you were trying to finish your book, it would probably put the final seal on it." She looked at him apologetically. "I suppose I was being a bit selfish. I was thinking of myself."

"I forgive you." He did.

"And then I suddenly had cold feet about the whole thing and imagined that you might be brow-beaten by her, or something like that. So I came out to protect you."

He sat back and stared at her. "And the whole thing worked out more or less as you had imagined?"

"Yes, it did, as it happens."

"But what about my thinking I'd fallen in love with somebody else altogether . . ."

"That was tricky," said Gloria. "But I think you dealt with that yourself. You did the right thing. So if that were going to be a test, you would have passed with flying colours."

"You're not saying it was a test?"

"Certainly not," she said. "Unless you decided that was what it was. For yourself, of course—a test you set yourself."

He shook his head. "No, I didn't."

"Well, there you are, then." She smiled at him. "I hope you felt the whole trip was worthwhile."

"It was."

He was going to say more; he was going to reflect on how he had been able to help, intentionally and unintentionally. But that would have been boastful, and good deeds should never be paraded by those who do them, no matter how strong the temptation to do so may be.

He looked at Gloria across the table. Sometimes the things that are most important to you are right under your nose and you just don't notice them. Then the scales fall from your eyes when you are away from home, in a small hill town in Tuscany, for example, where unusual and extraordinary things happen. And then you realise how rich life is, and how precious.

"Shall we go to Venice?" he asked. "I seem to recall your saying you'd never been there."

"I'd love to," she said. "When?"

"Very soon," he said.

"And you could do a Venetian book. A seafood book, perhaps."

"I can just see it," he said. *"Paul Stuart's Floating Table."*

He reached out and took her hand across the table, which she gave, willingly, and with tears in her eyes.

"I can't help myself," she said. "I always do this. I cry when I'm happy."

"Cry away then," he said. "And I may even join you."

"Could we hire a boat in Venice?" she asked.

He thought about this before answering. "I don't see why not."

And for a moment, in his mind's eye, he saw a working boat, a rough bruiser of a barge, complete with crane, moving slowly through the waters outside the entrance to the Grand Canal, and on the deck, or perhaps even at the wheel, two utterly happy people, their arms around each other, pleased at having found Venice, a boat, and themselves.